Sittin' 'Round The Stove

Stories

from the

Real West

Dedicated to
Dow & Karleen Overcast
They lived what they believed
&
Left us a clear path of integrity to follow.

Quotable Wisdom
Passed Down *from* Grandad & Granny

———◦◦◦———

"If it's worth doing, then it's worth doing well.
When you tie into something,
<u>always</u> do the very best you can."

"Whenever you have a little disagreement with
someone, always remember …
… the least said is the best mended."

Karleen Overcast
1902-1990

———————————————————

"I've never done anything in my life that I didn't
want to do. If I thought it would make me money,
I wanted to do it, and if it wouldn't …
… well, I just didn't do it."

"Buy the best land you can find.
It's way the cheapest in the long run."

"I've always tried to put my money where it
would make me a little back. That car ain't
gonna do anything but cost you money."

Dow Overcast, Sr
1902-1983

Photographic Credits

Table of Contents

Table of Contents

Table of Contents

Introduction

------⟨⟨⟨⟩⟩⟩------

*T*hanks for taking a look at *Sittin' 'round the Stove*. Here you'll find a fun little collection of short stories from the Real West. Our perspective out on the ranch in the middle of Montana gives us a perspective that is really becoming unique, when you consider the increasing urbanization of America.

So come along with me on a little trip. Let your mind wander a little bit as you join me on a few adventures. There's no real place to start and stop when reading this. Each story stands on its own. This is actually our fourth book of tales from the Real West, so if you enjoy it and would like to take a look at the others, there's contact information on the first few pages.

Some of these pages contain stories that are ... honest Injun ... 100% the truth, and a few of them may accidentally contain what someone has called "creative truth enhancement." There are a few that are little mini-biographies of historical figures that you may or may not be familiar with. Those are as accurate as I could possibly make them.

I owe a big debt of gratitude to my friend Gary A. Wilson, a noted author and historian for all of his help, and for graciously loaning me a few priceless photographs, just so I could share them with you.

So ... what are we waiting for? Let's just tie right in. Enjoy.

Ken

10

Chapter One

Straight As a String

*I*t started off like any other normal day around here. Please note however, that a normal day on this outfit would certainly not be classified as normal anywhere else. Only a certified nut-house graduate would consider anything around here normal.

Here's the deal: I needed to put some permanent irrigation border dikes in a field where we were doing some land leveling. Because they were going to be there forever, and that's quite a while, I wanted to make sure that I got them in straight.

Now, for the record, I'm normally not that picky. Oh, I try as hard as I can to get them straight, but if they've got a little hooey in 'em ... oh well, it's really not that big o' deal ... but these were long ... really long ... about 3500 feet or so. I tried the first one on my own, and it turned out as crooked as a dog's hind leg.

11

"Guess I'll have to go to the house and talk the cook into a little help," I says to myself.

Now just for the record, she's a pretty good sport that little gal of mine, but she sure got me in a mess this time. Here's how this deal went down:

"What do you want me to do?"

"I need to get those border dikes in the field straight, so I'll measure over on one end and drive in a steel post and hang somethin' on the top of it I can see for a long ways, an' then I'll measure over on the other end an' put in a little flag."

"So what do you need me for? Sounds to me like you've got it all figured out."

"It's too far to the other end. All you have to do is go down the field and I'll stand at one end and wave you right or left until you're right in line with the post on the other end and when I wave like this (I waved my arms over my head) you just stick one of these little flags right between your feet. There's nothin' to it. We'll just put in eight or ten flags where each dike is gonna go and they'll be straight as a string."

There was one itty-bitty problem. I've only got one eye and she ain't near as good as she used to be, and I couldn't see the post with the big red flag on the other end of the field. The binoculars worked great, but after my lovely assistant got a couple of thousand feet away, she couldn't tell if I was waving for her to move right or left.

We needed two pair of binoculars, and we've only got one.

Not to worry. "Necessity is the mother of invention," as the old saying goes.

"I'll just use the scope on the rifle," I ingeniously remarked. (Allowing my lovely little wifey to use the rifle scope while I used the binoculars was out of the question. I might be sort of dumb, but I'm not dumb enough to EVER let her get a bead on me.)

Being the chicken that she is, my little darlin' was certain that I'd probably shoot her, but I reminded her of the fact that I can't cook, and don't have enough money to hire one so she was safe as can be. I took the clip out of the rifle and checked a dozen times to make sure there wasn't a hidden bullet in there someplace, while my lovely assistant packed her luggage for the safari.

I don't honestly think she took a change of clothes (this time) but she had to have her sun glasses and a dozen water bottles and of course the sun screen, and an entire assortment of other things that ladies view as absolutely essential.

"For cryin' out loud, honey. We ain't stayin' over night. This isn't going to take more than a couple of hours."

"You want me to help or not?" came the calloused reply. (Foolish question - Obvious answer.) Sooooo....... I helped her load all the stuff in the pickup and out to the field we went, she was driving the pickup and me on the tractor.

The first couple of dikes when without a hitch. We were really gettin' the hang of putting those little flags in as straight as an arrow. Then things started to go wrong. A little bit wrong at first ... then, REALLY wrong.

All those "absolutely necessary" bottles of water the lady of our crew had packed into her little bag of tricks started to take their toll, and Mother Nature issued an extremely urgent call for bladder relief. Communication is fairly difficult when you're several thousand feet apart, and all I could see through the scope on the rifle was her jumping up and down and motioning wildly towards some brush at the edge of the field.

Of course, I had no idea what was going on, so I just followed her extremely erratic and speedy flight to the edge of the field through the cross hairs, trying my best to figure out what in the world was the matter.

"Maybe this isn't such a good idea," I began to think to myself ... (best I could with the gumbo in my nose.)

I think I forgot to mention another fairly important aspect of this little incident. We weren't over a quarter of a mile from the highway. Here's the best I can piece the rest of this story together:

14

1. Some kind of a law enforcement guy fresh out of cop school was cruising by.
2. He saw a lady running wildly for the brush, and a man with gun.
3. He called for backup, and then circled around behind the alleged perpetrator (me).
4. The tractor was running, and I had in my ear plugs.
5. I didn't hear him coming.

I learned some very important lessons from what transpired next that I'd like to share with you.

1. They really teach those guys how to sneak up on a fella at cop school.
2. Those billy clubs REALLY hurt.
3. That mace stuff is REALLY bad.
4. Handcuffs behind back, face in the dirt, combat boot between shoulder blades ... is not a good combination.

And perhaps the most important lesson of all:

Just maybe using the rifle with the scope in the field by the road isn't as good an idea as I thought it was.

"You know, they say some guys are a lot
smarter than they look. Unfortunately ...
that ain't always the case."

Chapter Two

Three Hundred Bucks Worth of Gangrene

*A*s the rain gently pattered on the rusty tin roof of their old porch, Dick and Billy sat contentedly, enjoying a couple of liquid barley sandwiches, and gazing out across their ramshackle kingdom. It was beginning to puddle up, and it looked like they'd finally gotten the three day soaker the range needed so badly.

"Boy, just look at 'er rain," Dick remarked to his old bachelor partner.

"Yea ... ain't that somethin'? If the weatherman could just figger out how to send us one of these a couple o' times a month, it'd sure make life a lot easier around here," Billy returned.

It had been a long dry spell and the rain had freshened up the stale dusty air as well as their worn out attitudes. The two old partners just sat in silence, enjoying the patter of the rain for several minutes before Billy finally spoke.

"You 'member the time we trailed those yearlin's down to that grass we rented in the Breaks, an' got caught in one o' these? I never been so cold in my life. That was three days of pure torture. Tryin' to catch some sleep under a jack pine all rolled up in yer slicker makes a fella wonder how in the dickens he ever got in a mess like that."

Dick just shook his head. "Yea, I 'member ... makes me shiver just to think about it. Can you even imagine where you'd dig up any help for a project like that nowadays?"

There was another pregnant moment of silence before Billy finally answered. "Nope, I don't. They just don't make cowboys like they used to. I was just thinkin' about ol' Joe Husar ... now there's a tough ol' bird. You 'member the time that thoroughbred mare bucked him off down there on Raglan Bench and he ran his boot through the stirrup? That old girl must have drug him a quarter of a mile before the stirrup leather busted on that old Miles City saddle."

"Dang good thing," Dick shook his head, "that mare 'd probably still be draggin' his bones around down there.

The steady rhythm of the rain on the tin roof and the effect a liquid brunch tends to have on a brain made for an ideal reflective atmosphere. Several more moments of time passed before Dick continued with his leisurely train of thought. He began to slowly shake his head and quietly chuckle to himself.

"Yea, he's a tough one alright. You 'member the time his appendix busted?"

"Nope," Billy looked quizzically at his partner, "don't think I ever heard about that one."

18

"Well, that was back in the early '50s sometime ... about '53 or so," Dick continued to slowly shake his head and chuckle in unbelief at his own story.

"It was around St. Patrick's Day an' ol' Joe gets a belly ache. Usually that kind of stuff clears up after a day 'r two, but this one just hung on until some of the guys thought maybe he ought to go to the doctor. So ... one of 'em loads him up in his '49 Ford pickup and they take off for town ... 'course, it's a hundred and ten miles to town, and they gotta go through the Bear Paws to get to the doctor."

Joe Husar in His Prime.

"The road was drifted shut up by Baldy, an' they had to chain 'er up and shovel their way through the snow banks. When they finally got in to Doc Almas, he figured out right away what the problem was, so they wheeled him into the operatin' room and took the dang thing out. His appendix was busted and he was full of gangrene …. would have killed a normal person … 'specially after shovelin' all that snow."

"When he finally woke up from the operation, he was still about half asleep, an' he could hear some woman moanin' in the room next to him," Dick was nearly doubled over with laughter telling the story now. "With all that moanin' goin' on, ol' Joe thought he'd died, and had wound up in hell."

Dick and Billy are BOTH rolling with the giggles now.

"Doc Almas was pretty upset an' got to hollerin' about those dumb cowboys that don't go to the doctor until they're about half dead. Joe jus' told him that when you live a hundred miles from town and you gotta shovel your way through the snow to get there, you jus' don't come in ever' time you got a sore toe."

Billy just shook his head. "Nope," he laughed, "they don't make 'em like that any more."

"The best part of the whole thing," Dick finished, "was that I heard him say that gangrene or no gangrene, he thought he could have weathered it, and was upset at 'em for makin' him go to that danged doctor."

"They made me stay in the hospital for over two weeks, an' that cock-eyed trip cost me three hundred bucks," Ol' Joe snapped. "That was a pile o' money in '53."

They don't make 'em like that anymore.

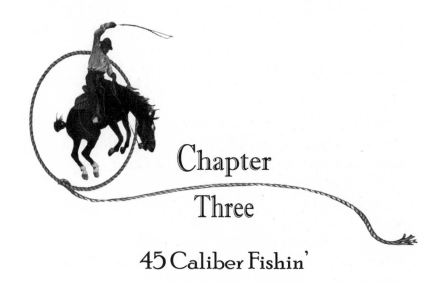

Chapter Three

45 Caliber Fishin'

"Who's it from?" Billy asked his ol' pardner Dick as he opened the letter freshly retrieved from the mailbox out on the county road.

Billy was behind the wheel of their old pickup bouncing down the rutted gumbo trail to their ramshackle outfit, and Dick was trying to make out what the letter was all about.

"Looks like it's from one o' my nephews ..." The bumpy road and the bouncing pickup made the letter readin' a little on the tough side. "... one o' m' sister's boys back East ... Andrew's his name ... looks like he just got outta law school an' took the bar exam ..."

"Bar exam???" Billy puzzled. "Why, I wouldn't live back there fer all the tea in China ... 'magine havin' to take a test jus' to go to a bar. 'Round here all's a fella needs is money ... an' you don't even need that if you got a pard 'er two."

21

"Not that kind o' a bar, you dope ... it's a test ya gotta take to git yer lawyerin' license," Dick returned as he read on down the letter.

"Lawyers oughta be again' the law if you ask me," Billy snorted as they rattled to a stop in front of their old shack.

Dick just ignored him as he read on down the letter. "... sez here that he's goin' to Alaska on a big fishin' trip, an' he wants to take us along ... sez he'll pay fer ever'thing."

"Yer kiddin'!" Billy exclaimed as he dug into the brand new twelve pack of barley sandwiches that they'd just gotten in town. "I jus' might change my mind about lawyers ... I think I'm startin' to like 'em already."

A couple of weeks later on a warm July morning the two boys and Dick's nephew, Andrew William Barkley III, were on a plane headed for Anchorage. Dick hadn't seen Andrew since he was a baby, and Billy was surprisingly sort of taking a likin' to him ... even if he was a lawyer. He figured that bein' raised back East like that, he probably just didn't know any better. Besides ... he was paying for everything.

They decided against choosing one of the fancy guided fishin' trips that were offered down by the river and instead threw in with Tommy Iglagook, an Eskimo lookin' guy that Billy had met in one of the skid row bars. Over several bottles of the finest illicit liquid refreshments that Alaska had to offer, they started to make their plans.

"I think we need to roll out in the mornin', an' get t' where the fish are by daylight," Dick slurred, his speech more than a little impaired. "You know where them fish 'er hidin' don'cha, Tommy?"

"Yea ... but it down the river. 'Bout four hours ... won't work to get up dat early," Tommy lazily replied, taking another big swig. "Fish don't even get up till nine."

The next morning Andrew and the boys headed down to the river right after breakfast, but they couldn't find that doggoned Tommy anyplace. About two hours later he finally came slowly and aimlessly shuffling down the path. Andrew was beginning to think that the hundred and fifty bucks Tommy had talked him out of as a deposit was a big mistake.

There were several boats tied to the dock, and the boys followed their trusty guide past several nicely outfitted and freshly painted ones to a rickety old piece of junk at the very end of the pier. If it hadn't been sitting in the water already, a fella might have thought it wouldn't even float, but by golly there it was.

Andrew was pretty upset with its dilapidated condition, but because the old boat looked like everything else Dick and Billy were used to on their outfit, they didn't even notice. Tommy climbed in and bailed several buckets of water out of the bottom, while the boys got the gear ready to load.

"Leaks a little," Tommy explained. "Gonna fix 'er one of these days."

They soon had the leakage all bailed out and the gear loaded. Tommy had selected just the right bait and had the fishing poles and the net completely ready. Andrew had on his brand new all-weather camouflage fishin' suit, and Dick and Billy had four twelve packs of beer.

"How come you brought that gun?" Dick questioned his pardner, eyeing the old Colt 45 strapped to Billy's hip. "We're goin' fishin', not huntin'."

23

"Ya never know when ya might need 'er," Billy explained. "Jus' in case ..."

Tommy pulled the rope and with a cloud of smoke and a couple of coughs the old antique motor sputtered to life. They were soon puttin' downriver, dribbling a hazy trail of blue smoke behind them, to where their faithful guide had assured them was the "best fishin' in 'Laska."

"Fish oughta be up by now," Tommy asserted confidently as he squinted up at the midmorning sun. The boys took turns bailing the fresh leakage out of the bottom of the decrepit old boat.

After three or four hours of puttin' and smokin' down the river, the crew had only consumed two of the twelve packs of refreshments. Captain Iglagook made a sweeping wide turn into a large pristine inlet of water. They were finally there!

Tommy instructed them on the proper way to bait the hooks and the right techniques to use, and soon all three of his clients were reelin' in the fish nearly as fast as they could throw the lines over the side.

Tommy spent most of his time bailing out the boat and taking pictures with the disposable camera that Billy had picked up at the grocery store when he was buying the necessary refreshments.

Things went great for a couple of hours, and then Dick landed a real whopper. It was nearly three feet long, and as they got it in the net and into the bottom of the boat, they noticed it was different from all of the rest of the fish they'd caught.

"Stay back!" Tommy snapped. "... Wolf Cod!"

Tommy's reaction was quite a change from his normal sleepy-head attitude.

It was about the ugliest fish a fella would ever see. It WAS nearly three feet long with a huge round head about eight inches across and a mouth about twice as big as his head; full of teeth that looked like sickle sections on a John Deere mowin' machine.

"Them 'er mean," Tommy cautioned, "awful bad to bite. We better jus' cut 'im loose an' throw 'im out o' here 'fore he gets us."

Dick is a brave sort of a guy normally anyway, and his liquid breakfast had added even more to his courageous nature.

"Ah, he don't look no worse than them Northern Pike we got back home. You jus' gotta get a hold of 'em behind their head an' ..."

That was the last thing that came out of Dick's mouth that was fit to print. As he reached his hand down into the net to take hold of that demonic lookin' fish, he discovered too late that Tommy really knew what he was talking about. They ARE mean, and they WILL get you.

Wolf Cod jumped two feet straight up from the bottom of the boat and with a snarl that would put the fear of God in a dead man, chomped that huge mouth full of sickle-section teeth down on Dick's right hand.

Billy never missed a lick. Without giving a second thought, he whipped out his pistol and squeezed off three rounds at that demonic fish. His aim was deadly. He put all three rounds in that ugly fish's huge head without hitting Dick even once; and they weren't exactly holding still either. It's hard to imagine how good a shot he'd be without a blood alcohol level nearing ten percent.

"There was one itty-bitty problem ..."

There was one itty-bitty problem. All three rounds also went through the bottom of the boat. I've never had the opportunity to take a scenic four hour voyage through the frigid waters of an Alaskan river with a finger stuck in a bullet hole in the bottom of a boat ... but I know three guys that have.

"Leaks a little," Tommy muttered under his kerosene breath as they pulled up to the pier. "Gotta fix 'er one of these days."

Chapter Four

Low On Ignition Fluid

*H*ere I was twenty miles from home in the middle of our summer pasture, and the dad-blamed pickup wouldn't start. Now, what in the dickens do I do? I'd been out tyin' up a little fence when it quit. (Some of my neighbors will probably be surprised to find out that I actually do that on occasion).

I very rarely go out there without draggin' along a trailer and a horse, but this time the object was fencing not ridin', so I was a-foot. I think everyone in the country has a cell phone but me ... I've been trying real hard not to get pushed and shoved into the twentieth century, much less the twenty-first, but I'll have to admit that one of those gadgets would have looked pretty good about then.

I was desperately trying to remember the smoke signals that Leon Limpin' Elk had showed me, but then I got to thinkin' about the results I'd gotten from the rain dance he taught me, and I kinda gave up on that idea. I've been dancin' that durn thing

27

all summer, and it dang sure hasn't rained so much you'd notice. I think my first mistake was paying him for the lessons in advance. That knucklehead musta took off to a Pow-wow someplace without botherin' to teach me the last couple of steps.

But ... because I'm convinced that the Lord looks out for children and idiots, it all worked out in the end. It was only a couple of miles over to the neighbor's and I'll be doggoned ... they were home. The Brinkman boys are pretty good mechanics, and they had me jury-rigged and the motor running in no time. Thank God for good neighbors.

When I got back home and the cook found out about my little difficulty, I was met with what seemed to her, to be the obvious solution to the problem.

"Lance (our son-in-law) told me he was afraid that old pickup was going to quit you," she asserted rather indignantly. "He said it was low on ignition fluid ... you SHOULD'VE checked it before you left! You didn't even check it, did you?"

The laugh I got from that one was worth the walk to the neighbors. I'm not too sure what Lance had told her, but I'm convinced it didn't have anything to do with ignition fluid.

Sooooo ... I went right in to the parts store, and told them that our old pickup wouldn't start and that my little wifey had sent me in for some ignition fluid.

"Sure," Dan the parts man grinned. "How much do you need?"

"I don't know. I've never bought any before."

"Well, that depends on how long it's been since it started," he added helpfully. "If it only failed to start once, you can probably get by with maybe a quart, but if it hasn't started for a long time it could take up to five gallons."

We've gotten more than a few laughs from that one. My little sweetie isn't what you'd call "mechanically gifted". But then she's not the only gal that's a little short in that area, and I don't think I'm the only fella that's "cookin' challenged". If she croaks I'm liable to starve to death.

Billy and Veda live down the valley a ways, and because Veda's mechanical ability leaves a little to be desired too, she dang near killed her better half a few years ago. It all began when the car wouldn't start. Billy backed the pickup around and hooked up the chain, and then talked his little darlin' into a giving him a pull.

Being the cautious type, Veda putted around the farmyard as nice as you please. Now this might come as a surprise to some folks, but pulling stalled vehicles has been the source of considerable marital discord on more than one outfit through the years. The old car had an automatic transmission and this little putt-putt routine of Veda's just wasn't going to cut it.

"For cryin' out loud, Veda," Billy yelled out the window, "take 'er down the road. You gotta get her goin' at least thirty five miles and hour 'fore she's gonna start!"

"OooooooK ..."

Out on to the county road she sped with her foot stuck firmly in the carburetor. Everything went according to the plan; the car started, the windshield didn't get busted and all was well in Paradise Valley.

Scene two of this little episode opened about a month later when the battery in Billy's little Farmall Model A tractor died. He had hay to rake and it was deader 'n a door nail. Veda's feelings were almost back to normal from the last towing job, so he braved his way back into the house to ask his little honey again.

29

This time he had the ton and a half truck all backed up to the little tractor and a short six foot chunk of chain already hooked up. After all, it should only take a short little pull. Veda was game ... again. Now, she's no dummy, and with the car startin' incident fresh in her memory, she already KNEW how fast you needed to pull something to start it.

Billy's rear end had barely hit the seat of that old tractor when Veda hit the end of the log chain. The resulting jerk is hard to explain to someone that hasn't been there. The death grip that the tow-ee had on the steering wheel was the only thing that saved him from landing flat on his back in the yard. Out on to the county road they tore, with gravel flying in all directions. Billy's screamin' at the top of his lungs and "Oblivious Veda" is catching another gear.

"We're only doing thirty," she whispered to herself as she glanced down at the speedometer and tromped on the gas, encouraging the old truck a little more.

The tractor started in the first three feet or so, but with no rear view mirror and no muffler ... how in the world was Veda supposed to know that? I must admit I've never had the opportunity to do 35 mph on a Farmall Model A that's hooked to the back of a truck with a six foot log chain, but between dodging the flying gravel and the floppy steering linkage, the visions this brings to mind will probably live on in Billy's nightmares for the rest of his life. The tractor started, Billy lived through it, and their marriage survived ... in spite of being severely tested ... again.

Just think of all the trauma poor old Billy could have saved ... if only he'd had a quart or two of ignition fluid.

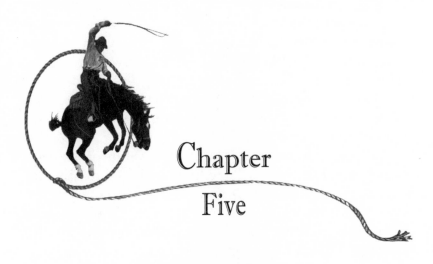

Chapter
Five

Ridin' An Old Trail

$\mathscr{D}$ick and Billy, the two old bachelors that ranch way out on the ridge, were just in town with a stock trailer load of dry cows last week.

"Market shore ain't the way she was a few months ago," Billy grumbled as one of their old girls went through the ring.

"'Course it ain't. We're SELLIN' ain't we? If we want to hit the TOP of the market, we've gotta be BUYIN'. That's just the way she works," Dick countered with his wisdom laden philosophy.

The boys both had a good laugh over that one, and then picked up their check and headed downtown for a steak dinner. They figure that a fella deserves at least that much before the banker scarfs all the money.

Over dinner, their conversation turned to old times and old friends.

"By the time we get back home tonight, it'll be too late to get anything done anyway ... whatcha say we stop out at the nursin' home and visit with ol' Barney a little. I b'lieve it's been four or five years since I've seen him."

"Yea ... me too. Sounds like a good idea to me. That ol' buzzard must be at least a hun'erd years old by now. It'd be good to see 'im again."

Barney Thompson was a cowboy ... one of the best, they say, but Father Time had been dealin' him bad hands for quite a spell now, and he'd landed in the nursing home almost ten years ago. The boys paid for their dinner, and then headed straight for the Home. They didn't even stop uptown for a little snifter first ... now, that's one for the record books.

They found a spot for their trailer in the corner of the parking lot, and were met at the door by a HUGE young nurse with a kind face.

"Looks more like a nose guard on a football team than a nurse," Billy whispered as she approached.

"I was thinkin' maybe we should see if we could get her to try out for the college rodeo team ... I heard they're short a good bulldogger." The boys managed to quiet their giggles before the lady got within earshot.

"Barney?" the nurse questioned. "You're here to see Barney? Well ... good luck."

"Whadaya mean good luck?" Billy questioned. "He's still here ain't he?"

"Well his body is ... unfortunately his mind isn't always on the same page as the rest of the world. He's got his good days and then he has his bad days. Come on, I'll show you where he is."

The boys followed her huge frame down the hall through the maze of impaired residents in various stages of physical and mental degeneration. There by the door to his room sat their old friend in a wheelchair, a red plaid Pendleton blanket covering his knees.

In a voice that was weak but clear, Barney greeted his two visitors.

"You boys lookin' fer work? Jus' got that train over there loaded with beef," he said motioning over one shoulder. "Sioux City ... that's where they're goin' ... think it's a mistake myself ... oughta be sendin' 'em to Omaha ... market's better in Omaha."

"Step down off yer horses boys," Barney continued. The boys squatted on the floor near his wheelchair. "We got lots more range to ride 'fore the snow flies. If you make hands I can give you a dollar a day ridin' for the Pool."

Barney's left hand was extended out in front of his body a little, and the fingers were spread just enough to let the reins from the imaginary bay gelding he was riding pass through. His right hand reached into where his vest pocket had been all those years on the range, and he calmly started rolling a one handed smoke, just like he'd done a jillion times before.

"Ain't no boozin' or cussin' in camp, boys. If you got a mind to hire on ... them's the rules."

Almost instantly the old roundup boss was transported to the open range that needed to be gathered, and the boys watched and listened in amazement as he called the riders by name and scattered them for the day's roundup. The names were ones from the past that they'd known, or at least heard of in old stories.

"Billy ... you pair off with Slim. If Slim can't make a hand out of ya, then there ain't no hope."

"Johnny," the old man called to an imaginary rider over by the nurse's station, "You take Dick with you ... an' don't kill 'im. He just might 'mount to somethin' someday."

With that final order Barney's voice sort of trailed off, and his chin slowly settled down on his chest as he drifted off to sleep. The boys stayed a few minutes longer to see if he might wake again, but that wasn't the case, so they began to thread themselves back through the maze of nursing home residents to the door.

"Good days and bad days," Billy parroted the nurse's words, looking at the hopelessness all around him.

"Yea ...," Dick answered, I'm sure glad we got here on a good day. I think maybe there's a little safety valve that the Good Lord puts in a feller's brain that let's 'em live in the past like that. I'd shore rather be ridin' an old trail ... even if it WAS only in my mind, than find myself stuck here in reality. This was a good day."

"Yea ... me too. This was a good day."

"Yea, I'd a loved to ride with them ol' boys. Johnny prob'ly <u>would o'</u> killed you though."

Chapter Six

Conflicting Bat Stories

*F*red and Mary live just down the road a ways, and I think maybe they could use a little councilin'. (Actually those aren't their real names. I've chosen these at random ... to ward off any potential threats of personal bodily harm.)

Often there's a little communication gap in this husband and wife stuff, but their deal has gotten plumb out of hand. There was a little incident over at their place not long ago, and the stories they tell describing it are so far apart that a Philadelphia lawyer couldn't figure out the truth.

Usually I'm up to almost any challenge, but my marriage councilin' career was sort of short, and even though I'm pretty sure they could use a little neutral party intervention, I ain't about to tie into it ... no-sir-eee, not me. (I'll tell you my marriage counselin' story some other time.) I'll just relate the two conflicting accounts exactly the way I heard them, and then maybe you can figure out who to believe.

It was the middle of the night, and the couple in question was sacked out in their upstairs bedroom. It was one of those hot nights with very little breeze, and the upstairs of their old farmhouse was plenty toasty. On at least this much of the story they agree.

Of course, they had a window open, hoping to catch a little breath of air if it happened by. Unfortunately Fred really isn't a very competent Mr. Fixit Man, because the window screen has had a hole in it for quite some time. We're not talkin' an itty-bitty "mosquito gettin' in" hole here, but one of those "Vampire Bat just walk in flat footed" kind of holes. Well, that's just what happened ... apparently. Here are the two versions:

Mary's story: "I heard something come in the hole in the screen, but I thought it was just the cat, (I TOLD you it was a big hole, didn't I?) but when I felt it brush my face on the way by, I soon figured out ... IT WAS A BAT!"

"FREEEEDDDD!" I yelled at my sleeping would-be protector, "There's a bat in here!"

"Fred is always hard to wake up ... especially if he has a smile on his face, so I gave him a good elbow in the ribs. When he finally did wake up and figure out what was going on ... did he rush to save me, his tender and dear wife of many years? Heck, no!"

"His idea of solving the problem was to rush OUT the bedroom door, push a chest of drawers against it, and then hold it shut so I couldn't get out, all the while yelling encouragement through the barricade,

"Get it Mary! Get it Mary! Get it Mary!"

"I finally did manage to get it into a garbage can, with absolutely NO help from Chicken Little who was still out in the hall holding the door shut. A lot of help he was. Sometimes I wonder what I need with a girly-man like that." (I told you counseling would probably be in order.)

Fred's story: "Night before last I was very rudely awakened from the best dream I'd had for ten years by this shrieking hysterical woman. She was elbowing me in the ribs with the covers over her head, yelling something about a bat being in the room. It took me a second or two to wake up and properly assess the situation. I must admit ... she was right. As a matter of fact it was the biggest bat I've ever seen."

"Mary ran from the room screaming and crying her face off and slammed the door behind her ... pulling the chest of drawers in front of it and leaning ALL of her weight against it."

(This part of both stories is sort of similar ... The only real question is; WHO is the party leaning against the chest of drawers in the hall?)

Fred's story continues: "That bat had at least a two foot wingspan, and the shotgun was downstairs ... I needed something really BIG and I needed it FAST. The biggest thing I could find was Mary's BVDs laying on the floor." ... (See what I mean about counseling? This boy's in big trouble.)

"After one heck of a fight, I finally got those huge wings entangled in that yard and a half of used lingerie, and managed to muscle him to the floor and hold him with one foot while I opened the screen. I then threw him out into the night with all

37

the strength I could muster and will never forget the sweet sensation of victory I felt as that bat was silhouetted against the full moon, trying desperately to fly away draped in four or five pounds of silk underwear. I then called out to my Mary to console her and tell the poor hysterical woman that all was clear and it was again safe to open the door."

Now just WHO do you believe here? Personally, I'm sort of leanin' towards Mary's version, but Fred will go to his grave denying that it has a shred of truth.

Here's my reasoning: I've never caught Mary in a windy, and Fred's been lyin' since he was a kid.

"NOW, can you see what we girls go through??"

Chapter Seven

Speed Komarek, Cowboy

*T*here's a tried and true way for a young fella to become a cowboy. I'm talkin' about a REAL cowboy here ... making a decent hand with a horse, and figuring out the complex psychology of working cattle ... of being in the right place at the right time and pullin' your own weight.

The secret is to find a good old hand that will let you tag along ... and then keep your eyes open and your mouth shut. The chances are pretty good that you'll learn somethin' if you've got your head in the right place.

Some folks say that energy is completely wasted on youth, and the wisdom of old age is the reward for not getting killed while applying all of that youthful exuberance. Most old cowboys can tell you a whole bucket load of tales that will make you wonder how they ever lived as long as they have. Speed Komarek made it more than 90 years, so I guess he must have been one of the lucky ones.

I wish I'd have been born just a few years after Speed, and then had the chance to follow him around in his younger days. By the time he died at that ripe old age, he'd forgotten more about cowboyin' than a lot of guys ever learn.

The name Speed's Mama gave him was Joe. He got dubbed Speed by outrunning a honky cow and the nickname stuck. He was born and raised in the Missouri Breaks, on the south side of the river near Armells Creek. His home range was a piece of wild rugged country that lies between the Cow Island crossing where Chief Joseph and the Nez Perce forded the river on the way to their last battle north of the Bear Paws, and down river to the mouth of the Mussellshell River to the east. The old outlaw trail used by Kid Curry and the Wild Bunch ran right through the middle of it, and the CM Russell Game Range now squats on some of the old open range country that Speed used to ride.

He just loved a broncy horse, and if he was ever afraid of one, he sure didn't let on. The wilder they were, the better he liked it. Many of his old compadres tell of horses so wild they had to throw them down to get the saddle on them. When they finally got that done, Speed would straddle the saddle, standing on the ground with a foot stuck in each stirrup, and then with a big grin he'd say, "OK, boys ... now let him up ... we'll see just how bad he really is."

His standard procedure was to get a hackamore and a saddle strapped on 'em, (by whatever means necessary) then only make a couple of circles of the corral before kicking the gate open and headin' for the cedar breaks.

40

"After twenty or thirty miles of explorin' that rough country, they weren't near as wild as they were before we started," he liked to say.

With range that big and rough, and the rides so long and demanding, the boys didn't ride colts like we do nowadays. The horses had to be at least five or six years old to have the endurance they needed. A honky wild horse and big rough country is quite a combination. It takes one good cowboy; the drugstore, barstool types need not apply.

It was April in the middle of the bountiful 1930's when Speed came into the house about mid morning. He was 18 years old and headed out to try to scratch out a livin' on his own someplace. As usual, he had run in a bronc, and gotten him saddled in the corral.

"Got a minute, Annie?" he asked his little sister. "I need someone to open the gate and let me out of the corral."

Annie agreed and Speed climbed aboard the wild knot head of a cayuse. As usual, it was a big stout gelding that had probably rarely seen a man, and NEVER had one on his back. After two or three frantic laps of the corral, Speed figured he had a good seat.

"OK, Annie ... open 'er up!"

That was April. They didn't see that cowboy again until he came riding back into the yard in October. I'm not sure if they even knew which way he was headed, or if he was dead or alive all that summer.

The picture on the next page graced the official Ceretana Flour calendar in 1951. It was taken at a rodeo in 1944 when Speed was 27 years old. As you can see, his hair was already fallin' out, so probably from a distance his bald head would make him look older than he really was.

41

Speed Komarek in 1944

He told me that he really didn't "hit his stride" on buckin' horses until he was passed 40, and I'm not sure when he quit riding the rodeos, but I've heard a lot of folks say that when he'd lose his hat on a wild ride, it was common to hear from the grandstand, "My! My! Look at that old man ride!"

There are a lot of us young bucks that fancy ourselves as cowboys. That's just because we're judging ourselves by the sissified times we live in. I think maybe we're more than just a little deluded, and in the old days would wind up as kitchen help (if we could make the cut). Here's another little example:

Sonny Smith happened by the Komarek outfit one day. It really wasn't just an accidental visit, as he'd taken a shine to Speed's sister Annie.

"Sonny, would you give me a ride in yer car?"

"I guess so," Sonny replied, with a quick glance at the house, hoping to get a glimpse of the dark haired beauty that was the object of his call. "Where ya wanta go?"

Speed explained that he'd bought three head of horses several miles away, and he needed a ride over to get them.

"They broke?"

"Not yet."

"How we gonna get 'em home?"

"I'm figgerin' on ridin' one of 'em," was the answer as he threw his saddle and some gear in the trunk.

Sonny's a good hand in his own right, so at least this time Speed had some help, but his helper wasn't really sure how they were going to pull this off. The two boys made the several mile trip across country, and found the horses right where they were supposed to be. They roped their front feet and threw them down, got hackamores on all three of them, and tied two of them up to the pole fence.

Speed saddled the one he'd picked to ride and made a few laps around the corral to "get part of the hump out of his back." Then the boys tied them head to tail in a string, Sonny threw the gate open, and his partner headed for home.

I'm pretty sure when Speed told me that story my mouth must have been hangin' open a foot. I'd never have had the guts to tie into a deal like that. It just looks to me like a wreck waitin' to happen.

"Ah, it ain't so bad, Kenny," he assured me. "If the one you're ridin' starts to buck, the one behind him pulls back and jerks his butt right back down, so when they're all tied together, they really can't buck very hard. Steerin' 'em, now that's another deal.

That outfit sure didn't turn very good, and 'til they got tired, the first few miles went pretty quick. Most of it was in the right direction, though ... we made 'er, OK."

There are a few of those wild old open range hands left, but not very many. Speed Komarek was one of the best, and I'm sure goin' to miss him.

Like a lot of guys from that generation, mechanical things just didn't come as natural as real horse power, and I'll never forget a ride he gave me in a car he'd recently traded for. He didn't quite have the new one figured out yet, and couldn't even get 'er started. After he finally got the motor running, he couldn't make it go anywhere and the old cowboy was getting more frustrated by the minute. No amount of lever pullin' or switch twistin' seemed to do any good.

He just looked at me in disgust. "Dad blame it, Kenny! If I could just get a hackamore on this &%#@ I could dang shore get us there."

"So long, Speed. See you down the trail."

44

Chapter Eight

Billy's Bedpan Conversion

"You know somethin', Dick," Billy reflected one morning at the breakfast table, "we've had a purty good year. We really got quite a bit to be thankful for." It was along between Thanksgiving and Christmas a few years back, and like most folks, the two old bachelor cowboys had been sort of countin' their blessings.

"Yea, you're dang shore right 'bout that," Dick returned as he reached for another flapjack. "Pass me some more o' that syrup, would ya? I can't ever 'member havin' this much grass. The cows are goin' into the winter fatter than they have in years. Maybe the Good Lord even smiles on cowboys now and then."

"Yea, the way I figger it, He's been smilin' on 'bout ever'body. The price them farmers are gettin' fer that wheat's enough t' make a fella even want to start diggin' in the dirt," Billy chuckled as he handed the

45

maple syrup across their ancient old table. "Just as well clean that up; we can get some more when we're in town today."

With that, Billy stood up and headed for the door of their old shack and began to put on his coat and overshoes, sailing the empty can of Milwaukee's finest (his usual breakfast beverage) into the thirty gallon barrel that stood in the corner. "If you'll clean up the table when yer done there, I'll go load up them dry cows. We gotta be headin' down the trail if we're gonna get to the sale barn in time."

In a half an hour or so the two old boys were rattling down the forty miles of bad road with six or eight cull cows in their dilapidated trailer. Their conversation on the way to town was filled with the things they had to be thankful for. Even though their ramshackle outfit maybe didn't look like a lot to other folks, they felt like they'd truly been blessed from above, and were discussin' things; like who they could maybe help out with the extra money they'd have with their dry cow check.

The chores, all those miles of gumbo road, and their natural tendency to just stick to themselves had kept them from ever goin' to church much, but they certainly knew the source of all those blessings they'd been discussing all morning.

They made it to the auction barn in plenty of time and had a good time visitin' with the neighbors as they watched the cattle sell. As was their custom, after picking up their check, they went downtown for a steak dinner and then just naturally drifted over to the Stockman Bar for a little snifter or two ... or maybe four or five.

Meanwhile, across town there was a crisis of sorts. Sister Mary Catherine, a spunky little nun that was

46

deeply involved in home health care for elderly folks, had run out of gasoline on the way to visit one of the ladies on her list. As her old car choked and died, she managed to coast to a stop on the edge of the street, only a block from the service station where she'd intended to fill the tank.

Sister Mary walked briskly down to the station to borrow a gas can, and then buy enough gasoline to encourage her car one more block. Unfortunately, the man at the station had just loaned his gas can to another customer, and didn't have a thing that she could use.

What a dilemma. She certainly didn't want to be late for her appointment. After all, the lady was counting on her. As she walked slowly back to her car, desperately trying to figure out how to solve the problem, the answer came! The little nun remembered the bed pan in the backseat of the car.

"Perfect! That should work just fine!" she thought to herself.

Her great idea put the spring back into her step, and she quickly skipped down the street to the station for a gallon of gasoline. I've never tried to walk down a sidewalk with a gallon of gas in a bedpan, but I imagine that the balancing act could be a little tricky. Sister Mary made it just fine, removed the gas cap, and angled the corner of the bedpan into the spout of her empty tank to pour in the precious liquid.

It was onto this scene that happened our two now VERY happy cowboys, definitely not feeling any pain from their extended stay at the Stockman. As they clattered around the corner in their old rattletrap

outfit, still counting their many blessings, Sister Mary Catherine had the bedpan nearly empty and was just shaking the last few drops into her thirsty gas tank.

"Whooaaa, Dick! Pull thish sucker over! Look-ee that!" Billy exclaimed pointing at the little nun.

Dick dutifully pulled over to the curb on the opposite side of the street about a half a block from the stranded vehicle.

"I'll be doggoned!" he slobbered in return.

"Lesh jush wait here a couple o' minutes an' see what happens," Billy gasped excitedly. "That beats anything I ever shaw. If that dang thing starts, I'm gonna be a Catholic the rest o' my life."

Chapter
Nine

Lookin' For the Orphan

Calvin topped a little rise while out checking his summer field last June, and decided to stop a minute to let his old pony blow his nose and rest his legs. It was a great summer day, with the birds tweetin' and not any wind to speak of. Those moments are really what make life worth livin', and both the cowboy and his faithful steed took a little extra time to drink it all in.

As they surveyed the rolling expanse of their kingdom, the perfect summer morning took a sudden turn south. Calvin's eyes fell on something that looked a little suspicious, nearly hidden in a patch of brush two or three hundred yards away, across a wide coulee. He urged his pony off the ridge ... and sure as the world ... there lay one of the bulls he'd turned out the week before ... deader n' a mackerel.

Now, that's the way to wreck a perfectly good morning if there ever was one. A close inspection didn't reveal any real clues either, so Calvin just laid the blame on a possible lightning strike and his seemingly ever present bad luck. But ... on the other hand ... looking on the bright side was always a trait around that camp.

"Son-of-a-Gun," Calvin grumbled out loud, giving the dead critter a kick. "Dang you anyway. Good thing we're a little long on bulls ... we oughta get by without you. Don't have much choice, I guess."

The rest of the ride went fine. Luckily they didn't find anything else out of order, and a further survey of the tall grass wavin' in the breeze and the fat calves soon made the loss a little more tolerable. The two weren't long making the rest of the circle, and were soon rattling their old pickup and stock trailer back down the road to the hay meadows that take up all the summer's spare time.

A week or so later, one of the biology professors at a local college called and asked permission to take her class on a field trip to "observe and document the flora and fauna present" in one of their pastures. Of course, Calvin agreed.

A few more days passed, and being up to his ears in haying, the field trip had been nearly forgotten. The haying crew had just stopped by the house for a bite of dinner when the phone rang. It was a college kid on the other end. Today was the day for the field trip and they'd managed to find a hill high enough that their cell phone would work.

"We found a dead cow up here in the pasture."

"Dead cow??!!"

"Yes. Miss Stangheller (the professor) says that we can determine by the life cycle and the species of insects present on the body that she couldn't possibly have been dead any longer than 48 hours. You need to come right up here. We're looking for the poor little orphan calf, but so far haven't been able to find one."

Calvin was dumbfounded. What in the dickens was killin' those cattle? He dang sure didn't have time to take off for the summer pasture again, but it looked like that's the way things were turnin' out. An hour or so later he had his horse loaded and they were rattling back up the road, leaving the neglected hay meadows in a cloud of dust.

When he arrived, there they were; a whole gang of college students following their professor around, just like a mama sow and her piggies, looking in every patch of brush for the orphan calf.

Bless their hearts, they WERE really trying, but they must have all seen the Bambi movie when they were kids. I guess they thought they'd find a starving baby with big eyes that would follow them anywhere.

What a wasted trip. Theoretically, there really WAS an orphan calf to find. Actually there were several, because by the strict definition of the term, there were probably quite a few calves in that field that had lost a parent.

The "dead cow" turned out to be the bull that had died a couple of weeks before. Most of the calves I've known don't seem to have a real strong emotional attachment to their fathers (if they even know who they are). Finding one that looks sad and dejected because their Dad just died might be a little tough.

I never did hear the professor's explanation concerning the discrepancy of the deceased bovine's stated time of death, but considering the fact she couldn't tell the difference between a bull and a cow … well, it sorta makes a fella wonder if it would be worth listenin' to anyway. We've got kids less than five years old around here that can do that.

Isn't higher education a wonderful thing?

51

"Yea ... you prob'ly don't know this Dick, but
I dang near went t' college once. After hearin'
about a deal like that, I'm dang glad I never."

"Yea ... I wuz thinkin' 'bout ...
maybe goin' into brain surgery, er somethin'."

Chapter Ten

Miss Apple Pie's New Shoes

*T*here are a lot of folks movin' out into the country here in the West that aren't really country folks. I really can't say as I blame them ... maybe a fella could get used to livin' in one of those cities if he really had to, but I sure hope I never have to try. Those newcomers can sometimes be a challenge to us natives, can't they?

Most of the problems come from just plain ignorance. After folks have been stuck in a little dinky city apartment without even a yard, and then suddenly have a whole three acres all their own, how in the dickens are they supposed to know it probably won't raise grass enough for their six new horses? Their foolishness is nearly enough to drive a man to drink, but most of the time they just don't know any better. They're out of their element and just don't have a clue.

Well, let me tell you something ... hay-seed country folks wanderin' around in the city probably seem just as weird to our urban cousins. When you take a country girl to the big city it might be a good idea to keep an eye on her ... 'cause chances are (if she's anything like the Miss Apple Pie that's been my travelin' partner since the Civil War) she won't have a clue about city ways either.

A few years ago my little honey and I found ourselves in Los Angeles. We'd recently published a new book, and the cows were all turned out on grass, so we thought we'd attend one of those national book conventions to find out how the big boys do it. I did a little research and found a name brand motel that was fairly reasonable in price and not far from the Convention Center, so I booked us a room and a couple of airline tickets, and off to LA these two country bumpkins go.

You talk about a couple of ducks out of water, we were it. We caught one of those shuttle buses to our motel that just by chance happened to be in a section of town affectionately referred to by the locals as "Little Korea". Most of the folks around there spoke a little English, although you had to listen pretty close.

The adjoining restaurant was run by Mexicans. Most of them spoke a little English, too ... but, not very well. How in the dickens those two diverse people groups communicated with each other at all is still a mystery to me. I think the whole outfit would have probably benefited from a good old fashioned Indian Sign Language course.

It was a nice room, and we got settled right in. Early the next morning, Miss Apple Pie, (my loving, but dangerously naïve little bride) went down to Pedro's to get us a cup of coffee. I should have known better than to let her out without her leash.

That woman of mine can strike up a conversation with a fence post, so when she didn't come back for a while, I didn't think a thing of it. Sure enough, she'd bumped into three young ladies to visit with in the restaurant. One of them was an Oriental, one was sort of Mexican looking and the third one was a black gal. As is the nature of a lot of country girls, she instantly made three new friends.

Miss Apple Pie
(with one of the neighbor kids)

"I love your shoes!" she remarked to the black lady.

"You do?" her new friend asked. "They only cost me fifteen bucks."

"Really? Where'd you get 'em? I want to get a pair just like 'em."

"Oh, downtown ... What size are you? I'll get you a pair when I'm down there today. I'm staying in the same motel as you ... just in a different part. You can pay me tonight when you get back from your convention."

So the deal was done. Miss Apple Pie's new friend was going to buy her a new pair of shoes just like her own, and they would straighten up the money later. Sure enough ... as we came back into the lobby of the motel that evening the Oriental desk clerk, (that we could barely understand), finally got the point across that he had some shoes in a shopping bag that a lady had left there for us.

"Boy, now that's something!" my little wife exclaimed, "that gal just met me this morning and here she goes out of her way to get me these shoes. I need to do something a little extra for her ... quick help me think. What can we do?"

"I know," she said (answering her own question) ... "I'll just give her one of your new books and take the money to her personally so I can thank her. I'm NOT going to just leave that money at the desk ... I need to really let her know just how much I appreciate what she did."

When my little dumpling goes back down to the lobby and informs the desk clerk of her intentions, he almost goes ballistic.

"No, no, no! You leavey money here, dat's OK! Jus' leavey money here! She tell me, jus' leavey money here!"

"Oh, no ... that will never do. I want to thank her myself. What's her room number? Just call her up and tell her I'll be right up. I've got a little gift for her."

The desk clerk is holding his head with both hands ... "No, no, no ... jus' leavey money here!"

If I had been there, I could have told the poor little man that I haven't won an argument with that woman in forty years, so he might as well give in.

He finally did ... but he INSISTED on personally escorting my little bride to her new friend's room.

They had to go outside the main motel building and across the street. It was now after dark, and in that seedy section of town, only crazy people walked around out there unafraid. They rang a little bell at the door and then entered into a hallway that, "wasn't near as nice as the part of the motel we're staying in." (Quoting my naïve little honey.)

There was a long hallway with six or eight doors on each side. When the bell rang a young girl's head poked out of each doorway. The emotions were probably a little mixed. Although they were more than likely happy to see their new friend fresh from the sticks of Montana, their hopes of the ringing bell being a real payin' customer, were obviously dashed.

The skinny desk clerk left Miss Apple Pie in the charge of the "Handyman" for safe keeping, and hurried back to the desk he'd left unattended. There in the middle of the hall stood the ugliest and meanest looking dude that little country girl had ever seen. He was a muscle bound, three hundred and fifty pounder that stood about six foot five. But, of course, her blue eyes and innocent grin even disarmed that big goon, and his huge pock marked face quickly returned her smile.

There in a room at the end of the hall my little sweetie found and properly paid and thanked the little black gal that had so graciously bought her the shoes. They had a nice (although brief) conversation

57

and the big goon escorted her safely back across the street to the lobby. (He was now her friend, too.)

Bless her naïve little heart. She still didn't know where'd she'd just been. I think she believes a Prostitute is some sort of religious group. You know ... like a Presbyterian or maybe an Episcopalian.

Personally, I learned something, too. I didn't know those gals spent that much time selecting just the right shoes. But then ... I guess if that's all you're wearing you'd want 'em to be really nice.

Chapter Eleven

Politically Correct BS

"*D*ang politicians!" Billy grumped as he fingered the newspaper at breakfast one morning. "The whole durn outfit's crooked the way she looks to me. Jus' listen to this," he said as he read a paragraph or two aloud. Dick was busy at the stove flippin' the hotcakes.

"One o' them guys is accused o' some kind of bribery deal, an' the other one jus' got caught with somebody else's ol' lady. What's this dang world comin' to? All they do is point fingers at the other guy an' try to get the heat of'n theirselves. I don't think there's a' honest man in Warshington DC.... that's what I think."

"Yer pro'bly right. Here ... have a couple of hotcakes an' cool down a little. Ain't no sense havin' a stroke b'fore six o'clock in the mornin' the way I see it." Dick flipped three or four hot cakes on Billy's plate.

Billy poured syrup on his flapjacks and started to eat, but it's hard to concentrate on breakfast when you're worked up over all the political flap. "If there's somethin' good happens they take all the credit, an' if it's bad they figger out how to blame it all on the other guy, an' ..."

His sentence just sort of trailed off over a cliff and Dick could see a little light come on way back in the ol' boy's brain someplace. It was something that happened so rarely that it was easy to recognize.

"That's it!!! Instead o' jus' complainin' about this deal, I'm gonna DO somethin' about it!"

"Yea? Like what?"

"I'm gonna run fer Congress 'er the Senate 'er somethin' ... THAT'S WHAT!" With all the excitement over his big idea, Billy was really shoveling in the hotcakes now.

"You a Democrat 'er a Republican? I've known ya fer forty years, an' I ain't even got that figgered out."

Billy's jaw dropped, revealing a mouth full of half chewed hotcakes. "You lookin' fer a fight 'er somethin'? You hadn't oughta call a man dirty names like that. I ain't NEITHER ONE! I jus' tol' ya ... they're all crooked. Big money runs ever'thing an' them guys are all cut out o' the same stuff. I'm a Independent ... that's what I am!"

Dick just smiled to himself and went on with his breakfast. After a long pregnant silence he finally spoke up. "Well, yer dang shore independent ... I'll give you that. An, big money definitely aint' got a hold on you, that's fer sure," He grinned. "Anybody can see that by them holes in yer boots ... an' yer sure a man of yer convictions. Once you get an' idea

60

in yer head, nobody could change yer mind with a sledge hammer."

"Laugh all y' want. This country o' ours is goin' t' hell an' what she needs is a good ol' fashioned grass roots can'idate on the ballot."

"Billy ... ," Dick erupted in laughter glancing down at the manure stains on his friend's jeans, "you give grass roots a whole new meanin'."

Just then the sound of an approaching car and the barking dog announced they had a visitor. It was one of Billy's nephews ... one of his sister's kids that had gone off to college.

"If it ain't little Bobby," Billy grinned. "Come on in an' have a hot cake."

"They call me Robert now, Uncle Billy," the nephew corrected. "I'm sure glad I got here before you ate them all. I'm starving."

They had a nice visit. Robert was just passing through on his way to a big job back East. The conversation finally got back around to Billy's consternation over the political affairs of the country and his new revelation of running for a federal office.

"That's great!" Robert exclaimed. "I've got a degree in Political Science, that's what I majored in at the University. I'm sure I can help! What this country needs is a good old fashioned grass roots campaign."

"That's exac'ly what I think," Billy retorted, sneering at Dick who was still tickled at Billy's stained jeans.

"OK ... , " Robert began. "Let's get a handle on just one of the issues. What's your opinion of the budget deficit and of deficit spending in general?"

"The gov'erment's gotta spend within the budget, that's what!"

"Where should we make cuts? Social programs? ... Foreign aid? ... Senior's benefits? ... The military? ... What's your opinion on pork barrel projects, and Defense Department kickbacks? ... What spending programs are essential and which ones have to go?"

Billy's face turned red with anticipation. FINALLY, someone really wanted his opinion. "I'll tell you what ... ," he began.

"Uncle Billy," Robert interrupted before he'd even gotten started. "The first thing you have to learn about being a politician is you can't say what you're really thinking. No matter what programs you say you're going to cut, you're going to alienate everyone in your constituency that doesn't agree with you. Sooooo ... the secret is to talk all around the question and never REALLY answer it. Then you need to find a way to blame all of the country's woes on your opponent. That's the proper approach to expand your support base and thusly gain more votes. That's the name of the game, you know. The one with the most votes wins."

Billy's face was really red now. He just sat there in silence for a moment with his teeth clinched. That was EXACTLY what the politicians in the paper were doing. Finally the reality of the situation soaked through that hard head of his.

"Maybe I ain't really cut out fer this after all," he resigned as he glanced down at the green stains on his jeans. "I think maybe I'll just stick to the BS I know a little more about ... at least it's honest BS."

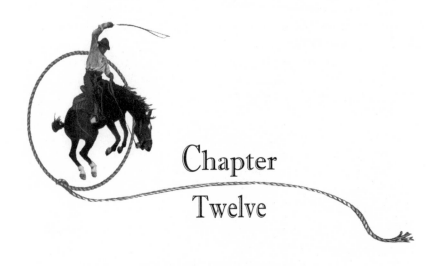

Chapter Twelve

Ferocious Feminine Revenge

It was a clear morning in the later part of summer a few years ago, and Diane was bustling around the kitchen finishing up the dishes, trying desperately to get a couple loads of clothes in the washing machine before her planned trip into town. There were twenty-five or thirty miles of gravel road between the ranch that John and Diane called home and the nearest little cowtown where they did most of their business.

Although the crew was getting towards the end of the haying, they were still running full speed ahead, trying to get it all done before the snow flew. I know it's sometimes a little hard to envision September snow banks when it's 100 degrees in August, but experience has proven that stranger things HAVE happened ... and the little incident that occurred on their place that day maybe helps to confirm that fact.

Glancing out the kitchen window, she could see one of the hired men headed to the field in the swather and another one with a hand full of wrenches by the baler in front of the shop. John was headed toward the house in that "runnin'-walk" so common to ranchers during haying time.

"Stop by the shop before you leave for town," he yelled in the back door, "I think we'll need you to pick up a few parts."

"OK," she answered with her head in the washing machine.

Although Diane was always willing to help whenever she could, she always dreaded the times she was asked to stop at the machinery dealer for parts. The parts man always seemed to ask a whole string of questions she didn't have a clue how to answer, and if she happened to answer one of them incorrectly and then came home with the wrong part ... well, it wasn't a pretty sight.

After a quick shower and a clean set of clothes, the faithful little ranch wife was finally ready to take off for town. She stopped the car down by the shop to see if indeed she'd have to be a "parts gopher" ... again. The second hired man and the hay baler pulled out for the field just as she got there, and she thought ... just maybe ... she'd get out of it this time. No such luck.

John was standing in the middle of the shop beside the four wheel drive pickup he'd been working on, with a whole list of part numbers scribbled on the back of an old paper sack. He could see the dread and apprehension in her eyes, and took this rare opportunity when they were finally all alone, to hug her up a little and give her a big kiss or two. It's sometimes amazing what you can talk your wife into with a couple of little smooches.

Well, she fell for it ... AGAIN ... and before she knew it, was on her way to town with John's parts list scribbled on the that greasy old sack.

Diane had several stops to make; the hardware store, the bank, the machinery dealer (of course), and the post office. She saved the grocery store for last. In this heat, she sure didn't want the ice cream and the other frozen stuff sitting in the car while she did everything else.

She didn't notice anything strange in the way everyone had greeted her ... at the time, at least. But in retrospect, AFTER she noticed the itty-bitty problem with her wardrobe, those weird and not quite normal looks she had gotten from the townsfolk made a lot more sense. The one that stuck out in her mind the most was the young woman teller at the bank whose face had turned beet red when Diane had walked up to make her deposit.

"That's a little strange," Diane thought to herself, as the teller seemed to turn away in embarrassment, "Cindy's always been so friendly in the past ... she must just be a little shy."

All of those strange reactions seemed to fall into perspective as she pushed her shopping cart past the big mirror in the grocery store. There right on the front of her new white blouse for God and everybody else to see, were two of John's big greasy hand prints. Apparently the little "lovin' up" he had given her to persuade his darlin' to pick up the spare machine parts had gotten a tad overzealous.

Diane was mortified. She had just been all over town, and everyone had seen those big greasy fingerprints on her blouse but her. She'd kill him ... that's what she'd do.

The closer to home she got the madder she became. Our heroine drove right down to the shop ... she'd give him a piece of her mind, that son-of-a-gun. The

65

air compressor was chattering away in the corner and the male perpetrator of the crime was on the creeper, back under the four-wheel drive pickup ... again ... with only the bottom half of his body visible, and the impact wrench pounding away. It was so noisy in there you couldn't hear yourself think, and John hadn't even heard her drive up.

Diane's mind was somewhere in that deep black canyon between uncontrollable rage and tears.

"I'll fix him!" she said to herself. With all of the strength she could muster, Diane grabbed a handful of whatever was available in the crotch of John's jeans and jerked it as hard as she could.

That was quite a shock to the jerk-ee. There was a howl of surprise ... and perhaps accompanying pain. The impact wrench fell on the concrete floor and our victim of uncontrolled feminine revenge sat straight up under the pickup. The rapid rate at which the injured party's forehead made contact with the transmission was the cause of considerable damage, (... not to the transmission ... it was fine), and ten stitches were ultimately required in the victim's forehead and right eyebrow.

This story has a couple of morals.

The first one: "What goes around, comes around." Although the retribution in this case was perhaps a little more severe than even Diane had envisioned, any ranch wife that ever happened to find herself in town in that poor lady's predicament would likely agree that SOME sort of punishment was in order.

The second moral: "Always look VERY closely before you jerk."

As Diane stomped self-righteously in the kitchen door, a glance back revealed a bleeding hired man staggering toward the house with both hands covering a fresh wound, and her dear husband John seated at the kitchen table pouring over a repair manual.

66

Chapter Thirteen

A Good Rhubarb Moment

Whenever we're travelin' around the country and have the time, we like to take the old back roads as often as we can. It's always an adventure, especially when you're not exactly sure where they're going to lead you, and the way I see it, it's the only way to really see what's going on.

I've always been intrigued with the old homesteads that you can run across on those trails ... especially the ones that have been abandoned for years. I've got quite a picture collection of decrepit old houses and ancient leanin' barns from all over the western states and Canada. I know a lot of folks probably just consider them junk that should be torn down and burned, but I see them as silent monuments to a dying way of life.

Every one of those old farmsteads once held a little family in its arms ... a family with hopes and dreams of a new life in the West. There were kids in the yard and clothes on the line, and a Mom and Dad with a lot more energy than money trying to hold it all together. Anyone with a shred of real rural experience knows the amount of blood, sweat and tears that goes into keeping a family operation's head above water.

The reasons why nobody lives there anymore are probably as varied as the old places themselves. Maybe they went broke for one reason or the other ... droughted out, hailed out, or grasshoppered out, or they could have just grown old and died ... the kids having moved on to dreams of their own. One of the neighbors may have offered them an ungodly price of five or ten dollars and acre for it, and it was just too good to turn down.

"We better take it, Ma ... remember what happened in '34. They can't never make a livin' payin' that kind of money. These land prices just CAN'T stay this high."

I read a statistic the other day that sort of shocked me, but it's one that sure helps to explain why we Western folks are like we are. Did you know about half of the immigrants to this country in the later part of the 1800's and the first part of the 20th century went back home to the "old country"? Well, that was sure news to me.

All of the sissies went back where they came from ... leaving only the tough, stubborn, and adaptable folks (and the ones that were too broke to buy a return ticket). The broke ones were forced to adapt or die ... so they adapted. Genetically speaking, our ancestors passed down those same stubborn, self reliant, adaptable traits to us. This sure explains a lot about our Western "never give up" attitude, doesn't it? (Not to mention the exact opposite mind-set of our distant limp-wristed cousins across the pond.)

There's something most of those old homesteads have in common, and I'm pretty sure it can teach us a thing or two.

RHUBARB.

Even after almost every other sign of human habitation has fallen down and rotted away, you can often times find an old rhubarb plant or two; still chuggin' away ... just like it has for a hundred years or so. While riding across new range in search of strayed cattle, I've often times come upon a rhubarb plant ... the only visible indication anyone has ever lived there ... until I take a little closer look around.

I think I read someplace that it's officially a fruit instead of a vegetable, but that really doesn't matter. The lesson we need to take to heart here is that, not only is the plant just as tough as whoever planted it all those years ago, but it has lasted after everyone has completely forgotten their family name.

In all of our striving to keep things together, it's sometimes hard to see the big picture. It's occasionally difficult to see the forest with all those dang trees in the way. Perspective ... now, that's the problem. It's a constant struggle just trying to maintain your perspective.

Keepin' the ranch together at the expense of the ol' lady and the kids isn't really good rhubarb thinkin'. I believe there are times that all of us tend to forget that.

We buried Ben Hofeldt a while back. He was a good cowman. A Bear Paw Mountain rancher that had put a good-sized outfit together and had all of his boys pretty well strung out when he pulled the plug for Higher Ground. He was in his 80's and died with his boots on ... fixin' fence; if all of us could be so fortunate.

A few months before he left us Ben had run across an old song by Tex Ritter called, "Take Him Fishin'", and he said that he thought it should be on every juke box in the country.

"Ever'body needs to hear that song," is what Ben had told a friend.

We played that old record at his memorial service.

Here's a man that had pretty much accomplished what he'd set out to do, but was a little concerned in his twilight years, that maybe he'd worked TOO hard ... and hadn't taken those boys fishin' quite enough when they were young. I've thought about that kind of thing a time or two myself.

We've got a little rented range that's a long ways from home, and Faith (an 8 year old granddaughter) and I just spent three days there, moving cows in the daytime and sleeping out under the stars at night.

As we were watching the big dipper circle the North Star, and her little head was resting on my shoulder, I was struck with the notion that this was one of those "rhubarb" kind of moments ... one that will last forever in that little girl's mind.

"God's pretty good to us, isn't He, Faith."

"Yes, He is, Grandad ... yes, He is."

Chapter Fourteen

Proper Baryard Etiquette

$\mathcal{D}$ick and Billy, the two old bachelor cowpunchers were floppin' down the highway in their old pickup and stock trailer last fall, when they ran into a gen-u-ine damsel in distress out on the road. They were headed home from the sale barn when they spied this little foreign sports car beside the road with a flat tire. I'll be doggoned, but standing there beside it, looking totally helpless, was about the best lookin' gal they'd seen in years.

Damsels in distress are a little hard to come by out West. A lot of times the girls out here are better hands than the men, so finding one that needs a little help out of a jam can sometimes be a real chore ... 'specially a good lookin' one. This was their lucky day. The boys were grinnin' from ear to ear ... they'd struck pay dirt. They rattled their old outfit to a stop behind the stalled vehicle.

"Howdy, Ma'am," Dick offered as he removed his hat and pushed a straggly lock of hair back, thankful he'd changed his shirt before they'd left for town. "Reckon we could give you a hand?"

"Oh ... thank you SO much for stopping," the lady returned in a rather proper British accent. "I didn't know what I was going to do."

Billy was standin' there all goo-goo eyed with his hat pinched tightly in both hands. It was obvious THIS gal wasn't from around here. She looked like she belonged in some magazine instead of standin' there beside the road in the middle of Montana.

"I think we can get you goin' again," Billy reassured her. "Just pop the trunk and we'll get at the tools and the spare."

It's a wonder that the boys even got the tire changed. They were so smitten by this dish with her little short skirt and cute English accent. Her name was Elizabeth Morgan, and she really WAS from England. It turns out that she had recently inherited a sizable Thoroughbred racing stable in Kentucky, and this was her first time to take a little tour of the rest of the country.

"So this is yer first time in Montana?" Dick questioned, lookin' first at his boots and then sort of sideways at Elizabeth. (She was way too good lookin' to just look at straight. A fella doesn't want to get caught starin', you know.)

"Yes, it 'tis. It's so ... it's so ... it's so vaaaast! Not a'toll like England."

She was very impressed by the rugged resourcefulness of the two knights in faded denim that had so graciously come to her aid, and of course, both the boys had their bashful old hearts all a twitter.

This chance meeting on the roadway of life began a friendship and series of letters that eventually led to an invitation to visit the Cunningham Stables near Lexington, Kentucky.

"Hot Dog!" Billy exclaimed as he burped down another complimentary adult beverage in the first class section of the jumbo-jet carrying them on their first ever trip to Kentucky. "Now this is livin'! It's hard t' b'leive that 'Lizabeth sent us them tickets ... 'magine that ... fer jus' changin' one itty-bitty tire."

"Yea ... it IS a little hard t' believe," Dick returned. "... an' I can't wait t' see all them high-dollar race horses ... but, then I guess money ain't no big deal if you got lots of it."

It wasn't long until the plane was on the ground. The boys were a little loop-legged from the slight over consumption of the refreshments, but Elizabeth had sent a car and driver to meet them at the airport, and soon they were shown to the guest quarters at Cunningham Stables.

"Holy shmoke," Billy slurred as soon as they were out of earshot of the driver. "Get a load of them chandeliers ... if this is the bunkhouse, I wonder what the big house is like?"

The boys had barely gotten their brand new shirts and jeans out of the suitcase when Elizabeth was at the door ... looking as pretty and proper as ever."

"Oh thank you soooo much for coming. I want so badly to show you the stables, and to get a real cowboy's opinion of some of our better racing prospects."

"We're ready," Dick offered.

"Yep ... lesh go," Billy added, holding the door for their gracious hostess.

Cunningham Stables was obviously a very high dollar operation. There were painted white fences

73

as far as you could see in every direction. Elizabeth was still very new to the horse business. She had been raised in an aristocratic family of privilege and educated in the finest private institutions in England, and with all of her goo-gobs of money, it was pretty hard not to look successful.

"These are the three year olds we have in race training," she offered as they entered into a long immaculately kept stable. Groomsmen and stable boys were bustling about everywhere. The horseflesh was the best that money can buy, and were a real eyeful. The boys were obviously very impressed.

"… and THIS is Royal Commander," Elizabeth stated proudly as they neared the box stall at the far end of the stable. "He is our leading sire. We have extremely high hopes for what he can do for our breeding program. We have his very first crop of foals this year."

He was indeed a magnificent animal. He arched his neck as the company arrived and wheeled around in his oversized box stall. He raised his tail in salute and graced the warm Kentucky air with the thunderous sounds and smells of a truly royal flatulence.

Elizabeth was appalled. This was very foreign and unacceptable behavior to her cultured upbringing. The boys were still admiring the stallion and really hadn't noticed anything out of the ordinary until she apologetically spoke up.

"I'm sooooooo sorry," the finely cultured lady entreated. "Please accept my apology for such crude behavior."

"Oh, thash OK," Billy slurred sympathetically. "… 'sides I thought Commander done that."

74

Chapter Fifteen

One Mad Mexicali Mama

I s'pose every one knows by now that smoking is bad for your health. That is unless the scientists decide to change their minds on that one, too. I really doubt they will, but it seems like every year all the smart folks that are supposed to know what's good for us make a big announcement that the very thing that was supposed to kill all of us last year is suddenly really good for you. Trying to figure all that out is enough to drive a fella to drink. (Is drinkin' good for you ... or bad?)

I never picked up the smokin' habit myself. It really didn't have anything to do with health concerns or any brains on my part. It's just that Lucky Strikes cost thirty cents a pack, and I was too tight to spring for 'em.

My poor ol' Dad smoked for sixty years and when he finally quit, it dang near killed him. I guess his skinny old frame must have been pretty used to all that nicotine, because he was in and out of the hospital for several months after he quit. It was quite a shock to his system.

Sheri Miller used to smoke, too. Of course, she listened to all the doctors that told her how bad it was for her so she quit. That's been several years ago now, and I'll be doggoned if she hasn't had asthma ever since. I guess it could be just a coincidence that the two things happened at the same time, but I really doubt it.

That asthma is bad stuff. It just shuts off your air and you can't breathe. Now, that's scary. Sheri's has been pretty well under control lately but there are times in the past that it's really given her fits. She'd tried just about every doctor and remedy she could find in an attempt to get a handle on it, but for a long time nothing seemed to work.

Probably grasping at straws, the Millers heard about an asthma and arthritis clinic in Mexicali, Mexico.

"What do you think, Lawrence?" Sheri asked her hubby. "I'm afraid one of those asthma attacks is just going to flat kill me. I know it's a long ways down there, but do you think we ought to give it a try?"

"We sure need to look someplace other than where we've been, that's a cinch," Lawrence agreed. "Maybe they can do something with my arthritis, too."

Too many years of hundred pound square bales had taken a toll on the old boy's back. I personally only look at cowgirls so I'm not much of a judge, but I guess you could say that Lawrence is sort of a handsome cuss. Lots of folks have said that he would have made a perfect Marlboro Man (back in the days when smokin' wouldn't kill you). He's tall and pretty well put together, and his dark wavy hair and black mustache really made him fit the part. I think he's several years older than Sheri, but he's still holdin' up pretty good.

So, down to Mexico they go. Mexicali is one of those border towns that we hear so much about. Everyone had warned them not to drive their outfit across the border, but rather to park on the American side and walk across and then catch a cab to the clinic.

Sheri tends to be a little on the excitable side. She's pretty much Irish, and unless my guess is wrong, Irishmen aren't really in the majority in Mexicali. She was scared to death, and was expecting Pancho Villa to jump out of an alley and get her any minute. Did I mention that stress and excitement tends to set off her asthma? Well, things were pretty exciting.

They finally found a taxi. It was a beat up '56 Cadillac with a huge set of antlers that had been borrowed from a longhorn steer tied on the hood. It looked like it came right out of the movies.

The cabby had a big suspicious smile, and Sheri was sure he must be up to something ... (kidnapping and ransom probably). The Mama Miller stress meter is pegged and her air is shutting down. Everyone was jabberin' in Spanish, she can't understand a word of it, and to make things even worse, Lawrence seemed totally unaware of the obvious danger, and was having a great time gawkin' around out the window.

Apparently miracles still happen. Within a few minutes the beat up old taxi with the kidnapper for a driver pulled up right in front of the clinic, and Sheri was sooooo relieved. Pancho Villa was nowhere to be seen either, but the excitement of the trip had caused a full blown asthma attack. She barely made

77

it into the building, and literally drug herself up to counter, fighting for every breath.

The receptionist was an especially pretty, petite, young señorita. Her dark hair was pulled up in the highest fashion, and perhaps just a little too much makeup really set off her dark liquid eyes. She looked a lot more like a movie star than a receptionist.

Sheri managed to gasp out what her name was and that she had an appointment. Every word was a struggle. The pretty receptionist was looking in her book to confirm everything, when Lawrence spoke up.

"See if someone can take a look at my arthritis as long as we're here."

Sheri ... (Looks healthy to me.)
The Mad Mexicali Mama

Apparently the pretty little dish behind the counter hadn't even seen Lawrence until now. She was obviously smitten with this tall handsome cowboy from America. She dropped Sheri like a hot potato and went right down to personally attend to her NEW customer. She was wiggling like a little puppy and battin' her pretty dark eyes, all the while striking her very best pose.

78

Sheri's breathing is sounding a lot like a brayin' donkey about now, and just standing at the counter was a real struggle, but being ignored while that little trollop was makin' goo-goo eyes at HER man was just about more than she could take. After all, SHE was the one with the appointment, and to make matters even worse, Lawrence (a red blooded American boy), was just eatin' up all the attention he was getting from that cute little dish of hot sauce.

Unfortunately, that wasn't the end of the story. With a sensual little wiggle, Miss Mexico handed Lawrence a couple of clip boards.

"Pleeze feel out theeze papers, Mr. Meeellar," she gushed with her eyelids fluttering.

Lawerence ... (Looks innocent.) The reason Miss Mexico nearly got an Irish whuppin'.

"There eese one for you," and motioning with a slight nod of her perfectly coiffed head to the wheezing Irish lady at the other end of the counter, "and theese one eese for your mother."

Oh, boy. A word to the wise here; DON'T torque off Sheri Miller. That asthma attack was the only thing

79

that saved that little babe's life. Miracles DO still happen. Just think, if it wasn't for asthma, Sheri 'd probably be doing twenty to life in a Mexican jail right now.

They sat down to fill out the papers. Lawrence could hardly contain himself.

"Did you hear what she said?" he whispered.

Sheri ignored him. A faint wisp of smoke was slowly curling up out of her ears.

"Did you hear what she said?" a more brave than smart Lawrence asked again.

Sheri ignored him again as she took a mental inventory of her physical condition to see if she could muster the air to jerk that little waif over the counter and administer a good old fashioned Irish whuppin'.

Poor Lawrence ... if only he had the sense to keep his mouth shut.

"Did you hear what she said?" he queried for the third time, with a big grin.

"Yea," his loving and much younger better half finally snarled through clenched teeth. "I heard her all right."

You could have cut the air with a knife. But yes, miracles DO still happen. Lawrence was very fortunate that his Irish sweetie could just barely breathe, or she would have probably pounded him AND little Miss Mexico.

"If I'd a been your mother," she wheezed, "I'd a DONE something with you."

"Besides," Sheri glared at her dark handsome mustachioed hubby, "the only reason she likes you is 'cause you look like a dang Mexican."

Chapter Sixteen

No Sense Payin' For Something Free

They just don't make horse traders like they used to. Looking back a few years when both the supply and demand for horse flesh were at a lot higher levels, there were a few enterprising individuals that really excelled at their trade. Some of those ol' boys really knew their business. One of the names that was always considered synonymous with horse tradin' in the southeastern corner of Montana and the two Dakotas was "Heavy" Lester. There are several stories that have been passed down about "Heavy" that sure bear repeating. I think I'll tie into one of them.

Heavy's given name was really Avon, but he preferred his nickname. In fact, most folks didn't even know what his real name was. He was a stocky, good sized man, which probably earned him his name way back when, and he dang shore knew one end of a horse from the other. His base of operations was 25 or 30 miles southeast of Baker, Montana, but his reputation as a horseman spread far and wide. If anyone had a horse to get rid of (flaws and all) they got a hold of Heavy.

The world famous Miles City Buckin' Horse Sale is over 50 years old, and Heavy furnished the horses for the very first one, trailing a couple hundred rank broncs over a hundred miles to the first big doin's. It's been going ever since.

There was an old German farmer from the Plevna country that had a team of horses that he couldn't handle, so (of course) Heavy was summoned to take a look at them. Boy, he sure liked what he saw. They were a chunky set of dapple grays that were matched perfectly. They were as young as they were pretty. They just had one itty-bitty problem. The old farmer had let them run away a time or two and he was afraid of them.

I'm a little fuzzy on the details of the trade, but Heavy eventually wound up with a dandy looking young team of horses that were a little bad to take the bits and run away. You can bet your life that, because the old farmer was anxious to get rid of them, the price was probably right.

Years ago, there was quite a horse market in Chicago, and this team wound up in a bunch that Heavy put on the train to sell in the Midwest. In Chicago, if you represented the horses as a "broke team" you were required to harness them and then drive them around a square track. It was a lot like a race track, as there was a fence on both sides of an alleyway, except that the corners were square.

A Jewish businessman from the Chicago area bought the team, and wanted to see them harnessed and driven. They appeared gentle as kittens, and the businessman was obviously impressed with the way they looked and traveled. With Heavy on the lines and the perspective buyer in the wagon behind him, down the track they started.

Knowing their propensity to grab the bits and run, our driver and horse trader par-elegance was careful to keep them under control. Being a big man, he certainly didn't have the problems controlling them that the old farmer had, but definitely didn't want to take any chances on losing the sale.

"Let me see dem tdot," the demanding buyer urged.

Heavy knew they'd run if they got a half a chance so he very gingerly urged them into a trot for a short distance and then pulled them back into a walk again.

"Make dem tdot some more. I need to see dem tdot."

That gray team was a lot like dynamite. It looks really innocent too ... until it goes off. The horses were acting like they were born broke, and although he was afraid things might get out of hand, he reluctantly urged them into a trot for a second time. Much to his relief, they were perfect and he soon had them strung out flawlessly, and then as quickly as possible, back into a nice brisk walk.

"I need to see dem lope ... make dem gaddop," the demanding Jewish buyer ordered.

This was a recipe for disaster, and Heavy knew it. He put it off as long as possible, urging the team into

83

a trot briefly and then back into a walk again, while all the time using his very best salesmanship to try to close the deal without having to make them lope.

"I NEED to see dem gaddop ... make dem lope."

Finally he couldn't put it off any longer, and Heavy urged them into a slow lope. That was all the encouragement the gray mare needed, and her partner was just as willing as she was. They took the bits and headed back to Plevna as hard as they could go.

With his feet firmly braced and his powerful arms pulling back on the lines, Heavy was doing all he could but there was a square corner dead ahead and things were NOT lookin' good.

The very demanding Jewish businessman's countenance was instantly transformed from being a man in total control to one that was scared half out of his wits.

"I vont off dis vagon!!! ... I vont off dis vagon!!! ... I vood give a hundrdt dollors to get off dis vagon!!!"

Heavy, was blessed with both a sense of humor and the experience to see the impending doom. Not only was his sale down the tubes, but with one look at that square corner arriving at forty miles an hour, he could see that pain and suffering were mere seconds away. With his huge arms pulling back on the runaway team for all he was worth, he glanced back over his shoulder at the fancy pants businessman in his new three piece suit and hardboiled hat, spread-eagled in the wagon box and hanging on for dear life.

"No sense payin' for it. Jus' hold on about four more jumps an' you can get out fer free!"

84

"Yea, that Heavy was quite a guy. That's where
we got Ol' Cupcake here, ain't it Billy? Too bad
he ain't with us anymore. Come this Fall we
could use a couple more jus' like 'er."

"Mary had a little bum lamb
Raised him on milk replacer
An' ever' place that Mary went
The dad-blamed thing would chase 'er

It chased her plumb to school one day
The teacher's mad as hops
Mary 'r the wether had to go
So now he's mutton chops"

(That's how that story goes ain't it?)
86

Chapter Seventeen

The Three SOB Rule

This ranchin' deal is a team effort in most cases. I've got a few ol' bachelor partners that seem to get by OK all by themselves, and a few neighbors who's ol' ladies work in town (and ain't any help when they are home ... except for their pay check), but for the most part, the outfits I'm most familiar with are pretty much a family affair.

Just STAYIN' married to the gal you work cows with is a challenge. The times when relations got the most strained around here were all a result of both of us trying to get too much done with too little time, help, and money.

The closest I ever came to lowerin' the boom on my little darlin' was when she called me a dirty name when we were workin' cows. Oh no, it wasn't a cuss word. She called me by the first name of a neighbor that's known far and wide for his violent, childish temper. Luckily for us both, it happened right as she quit the operation and left me there to figure out how to try to get it done by myself.

We bought some short term stock cows a few years ago, and (as is usually the case) inherited every old reprobate within 150 miles of here. We had wild ones, fence climbers, bad bags, you name it. I think the word must have gotten out on the cow trader's hotline; "Overcast is in the market for some cheap old cows, so bring your junk to town."

As we were trying get a brand on them (in the rain) before we turned them out, this one old rip had gotten back on my little bride a couple of times. That's always a good starting place for a potential domestic dispute. The females of our species (at least the one at our house) tend to be a little less inclined to stand their ground with a honky cow, and I was gently trying to point this fact out to her from my position manning the empty squeeze chute.

"Don't let her get away with that! Crack 'er between the ears with a club she'll stop! Doggone it Ma ... you just let 'er go again! How come you moved? You jus' LET her get by you!"

It's probably fortunate that I don't recall the response I received from my little darling on that fateful day. I'm sure it would be unprintable anyway. The gist of her communication was that SHE'D run the chute and I could get run over by that old bag if I wanted to.

I was all too happy to show her how it needed to be done. "Piece o' cake," I thought to myself.

Unfortunately for the pecking order in our family ... she was right. I got freight-trained and wound up with a perfectly coordinated wardrobe; Cow manure on the back & cow tracks on the front. (Being a chicken does sometimes have its place.)

I know our outfit isn't the only one that is maritally challenged when the goin' gets a little rough. One of our neighbors locked his little darlin' in a steel grain bin one time when they got into a little "discussion" while they were sackin' up some grain. She's sort of the excitable type, and I guess he figured she needed a little time to cool off. I wouldn't be surprised if he sent one of the kids over to let her out. Being within "rock throwin' range" himself could have proven to be fatal.

Machinery is sometimes another sore spot around here.

"Would you run down and get the tractor and give me a pull?"

"How do you start it??? ... I forgot."

"The same &*%$ way it's started since 1977 when we bought it!"

(This was a VERY bad answer on my part, and led to considerable strife. I only included this to show you how NOT to do it.)

My little darlin' and I are working on our forty second year of marriage. Although she may tie a can on my tail tomorrow, at least as I write this I feel like sort of an expert in negotiating the minefields of agricultural married life. Not long ago we were visiting with another ranch couple (with a similar, sometimes rocky but overall successful track record), and we came up with a couple of rules to transform this art of marital longevity into a little more of a science.

Gary and Margaret have nearly 40 years in. Gary merely overlooks the fact that Margaret is "trailer-backing-up challenged" and that their stock trailer can no longer boast of any fenders without the red paint of town fire plugs, or the scrapes of corner posts.

Margaret, on the other hand has devised what she calls her "Three SOB Rule". This little rule of Margaret's has served them well, and is something I think the female members of our opposite sex should consider. It goes like this:

When her normally mild mannered and soft spoken hubby gets a little frustrated (for instance when they're working cattle and his generally very domesticated vocabulary starts to degenerate), the "Three SOB Rule" always applies.

"Hey ... come back! Where you goin'?" Gary calls to his bride as she's makin' a bee line back to the house.

"You said it three times ... I'm out o' here!"

"But ... but ... but ... it wasn't directed at YOU!"

"It doesn't matter ... Three times and I'm gone!"

That sounds like a pretty good frustration meter to me. Gary and I went on to discuss the increasing marriage failure rate, and I think maybe I've got a handle on at least part of the reason.

"The problem is just these modern men," I asserted confidently, making certain my little honey was out of earshot. "They've just never learned to take orders like you and I have."

Chapter Eighteen

Albert's Fresh Milk Cow

$\mathcal{D}$ick n' Billy had hauled a critter or two into the sale barn about this time last year, and because they hadn't been off the place for a couple of months, they headed right up town to wash down a little of the accumulated trail dust. Just bein' neighborly, they nodded and spoke to the ol' boy that was sittin' down at the end of the bar by himself, but by the time their eyes finally got adjusted to the dim lights of the place, they figured out he wasn't really someone they ought to know.

Come to find out, he was a stranger from back in the farm country of Minnesota, and had just drifted in ... and was lookin' for work. He said his name was Albert Burnham and he sure needed a farmin' job ... said he'd been a cook in the Navy, too.

There's not much that will perk the ears up on a couple of old bachelor cowboys like someone that wants to do the farmin' ... and the cookin', too. The boys had a nice visit with their new found friend over a couple of Milwaukee's finest barley sandwiches, and it wasn't long until they struck up a deal. There were a couple of hay meadows that sure needed workin' up, and sitting out on that dusty old John Deere Model R wasn't something Dick or Billy either one considered the top job on the outfit. Besides, they wanted to see if he really COULD cook.

After a quick trip to the store for a pickup load of groceries (just in case winter decided to set in) they pointed their outfit south, down the 40 miles of dirt road to the ranch. Albert tied right into the farmin' and doggone it, but he could actually cook, too. Now, he really wasn't the cleanest fella you've ever seen, with his month's worth of shaggy whiskers and the snoose drippin' off his chin, but he dang sure made a mean pan of biscuits.

"If I just had a little fresh milk, this stuff would all turn out a lot better," Albert would say about twice a day as he was measurin' out the powdered stuff from a box. "I can't understand how come an outfit plumb runnin' over with cows like this ain't even milkin' ONE of 'em."

Dick and Billy both just tried to kid him out of his grumpy little fits, while at the same time completely ignoring the snoose dribbling in the gravy.

"The biscuits 'd raise higher, an' this gravy 'd be a whole lot better, too. If you want some REAL biscuits and gravy fer Christmas, we've just GOTTA have some real milk.

"Never was much fer milkin' m'self," Billy would return on occasion.

"Me neither," Dick added.

"Jus' git 'er in, and I'LL milk her myself," Albert snapped. "I've milked a lot of 'em, and one more probably ain't gonna kill me!"

It was along about Thanksgiving sometime, when Billy was riding down through some of the dry cows and found an old Hereford-cross cow down in the brush trying to have a calf and not having any luck. He knew they had a couple of old girls in the bunch that looked like they were going to calve, but he sure wasn't banking on what he found that afternoon.

The calf was tangled up and stuck, and Mama was on the fight ... big time. She had a pretty good set of antlers on her, too and was backed against a cottonwood tree, pawing the dirt and shaking those horns in the air ... in total defiance of the guy just trying to lend her a hand.

Billy decided to trail her down to the barn, and put her in the big tall round corral to help her deliver her baby. The old girl apparently didn't even vaguely appreciate the fact that he was saving her life. She was trying her level best to tear the whole outfit apart.

After getting her snubbed up to one of the big posts, Billy straightened the tangled legs on the calf and after considerable effort, finally completed his mid-wifery chores. Unfortunately, the baby was already deceased ... and, if it's possible, Mom's attitude had degenerated even further.

As luck would have it, Billy had used a rope with a quick release hondo on it, so turning her loose again was a breeze. He just stood on the outside of the corral and reached through the ash poles to snap her loose. The wild old biddy jerked free in defiance and made a couple of laps around the pen looking for an escape hole.

It was then, from his safe vantage point on the outside of the pole fence that Billy finally noticed just how unique her horns really were. They were huge, and both turned naturally forward and upward. What made them distinctive was that the left one curled back to the inside, almost like a horn you'd see on a big horn ram. It didn't quite make a full curl, but almost. She had a nice big bag, too.

"Doggone shame," Billy thought to himself as he headed to the house to wash up. "She'd be a dang good mother if that calf had o' made it. No coyote is gonna get a baby of HERS."

Albert was seated next to the stove, with a book in front of his nose when Billy shuffled in the door. He'd apparently missed all the action down by the barn.

"Well, I got the milk cow in," Billy offered, trying to keep a straight face. "She just freshened, and the calf didn't make it. If you want some o' that fresh milk, all you gotta do is go an' get it."

Albert could hardly believe his ears. "… and here all this time I didn't think they were even listenin' to me," he thought as he grabbed the bucket and headed for the corral. Albert was a tall, long armed man with a sleepy sort of angular gait, and he snoozed his way right up to the huge gate with the log chain latch, and let himself in, paying no particular attention to the cow in the pen.

With his mind still on the book he'd been reading, he latched the chain behind himself and in his usual awkward manner, lumbered toward the cow. Unfortunately her attitude hadn't improved an ounce, and by the time Sleepy Albert saw what was on her mind, it was too late. He turned to run for the corral fence, with the bellowing deranged cow hot on his trail.

The first hook she made at the seat of his pants, the old heifer caught the bail of the milk bucket in the curl of that weird left horn of hers, and there

94

it stuck ... banging her on her already frustrated head. Meanwhile, the sharp pointy part of the right horn made a connection right around her victim's hip pockets someplace. Albert was now fully awake with his long legs making strides across the pen that would put a thoroughbred race horse to shame. It was somewhere near this juncture in the altercation that he swallowed his snoose.

After what seemed like a week, Albert finally made it to the corral fence, but even with considerable assistance from the "milk cow" (with the bucket still banging her on the side of her head), he didn't have much luck in climbing the old ash poles as they just kept spinning and rolling as he desperately tried to gain traction.

He finally made it to safety on the far side of the fence. In a triumphant act of defiance, the bellowing cow violently shook her head sending the milk pail whirling over the poles behind him. Her deranged eyes glared through the corral slats, coldly watching her victim limp to the house. Albert's clothes were in tatters, and horn marks decorated a generous portion of his exposed hide.

"You want that cow milked, you're gonna have to milk her herself." Albert declared as he drug himself into the porch.

Dick and Billy were both seated at the table, biting their lips in an attempt to hide their submerged laughter. Neither of them answered. Albert washed up and began to put the supper on the table that he'd left to warm on the stove. The next several minutes were spent in silence as none of the three men spoke.

Finally, Dick took a couple more biscuits. "You sure make good biscuits, Albert."

"Yea, they shore are," Billy chimed in. " ... but if we want some REAL biscuits and gravy fer Christmas, we've just gotta have some REAL milk.

"Never was much fer milkin' m'self," Dick offered.

"Me neither," Billy returned with his eyes on his plate, still biting his lip.

There was another long pregnant silence before the boys got their response.

"Well, maybe that powdered stuff ain't so bad after all," Albert grumbled, reaching for another biscuit. "I've milked a lot o' cows ... but, one more just MIGHT kill me!"

Chapter Nineteen

Jim McCoy, Old School Cowboy

*A*s a fella goes through life there are a few things we all do we probably wish we hadn't, and then there are others we'd perhaps like to take a crack at that just never seem to happen for one reason or other. Personally, I really wish I'd had the chance to visit with Jim McCoy. After all, he lived in the same neck of the woods as I do, but regrettably he rode over the "Great Divide" a few years before I was born.

Jim was an old school cowboy that came up the trail from Texas, and the stories he could tell of every day life on the open range would be worth a fortune. James McCoy was born August 9, 1862 at Burnett, Texas where his parents were among the earliest pioneers of the Lone Star State. Growin' up around horses and cattle, he continued his education by signing on with a trail herd headed up the Chisholm

Trail with a herd of longhorns bound for Wyoming Territory in 1876 ... at the ripe old age of 15. Kids seemed to grow up quite a little faster in the old days for some reason.

The next few years were spent in the saddle, looking at the rear ends of cattle all over the West. When he and his compadres arrived in the Salt Lake

Jim McCoy circa 1883

country behind a herd of cattle they were obviously wearing several months of trail dust, and were surprised to find that when they stripped down and dove into the lake for a badly needed bath they just floated around when the salty water buoyed them up. He also got a first hand look at the marvels of the Yellowstone geysers long before it was an official Park, and even spent some exciting time in Dodge City, perhaps the most infamous of the Kansas railhead towns. (It could be that some of the antics of those early years might possibly have been classified as Top Secret.)

Jim spent the famous killing winter of 1886-'87 in the Black Hills of South Dakota. It was that harsh winter which inspired the picture by our own Montana artist Charles M. Russell entitled, *Waiting for a Chinook* or *The Last of the Five Thousand*, as it is sometimes called. The severe blizzards completely decimated the cattle numbers on the northern plains, and Jim eventually arrived in Montana with a trail herd to help restock the empty range. He was following a bunch of cattle bound for the Milk River country on what is now the Fort Peck Indian Reservation.

After spending several years ridin' around the West, Jim McCoy finally settled permanently in northern Montana, working as foreman for many ranches and eventually settling in as cowboss on Colen Hunter's YT Ranch south of Havre. The YT was later acquired by Ed Redwing in 1911 and passed down through one of his daughters to the Solomon family.

Jim found a lady to take his name, and he and Mina Dowen, a new transplant from Michigan, were married in Fort Benton in 1896. Their home on the YT was one of the first ranch houses in the country to actually sport a wooden floor in place of the usual dirt variety.

Like many of his open range contemporaries, Jim was a man of few words but certainly had a few stories that would be worth a good listen. He always wore a handlebar mustache, saying that very few men on the range wore full beards, "... because they were too warm and tended to house too many four to six legged varmints."

He preferred stripped pants, held up with suspenders and wore his nickel plated Colt low on his right hip. Perhaps because he was also a State Stock Inspector for many years, Jim continued to carry his pistol long after most range cowboys had forsaken the practice. It was just a part of who he was. Jim strapped on his gun belt every morning right after he pulled on his boots. His position as a Stock Inspector took him far and wide across the State of Montana.

The McCoy's eventually bought a house and settled in Chinook, with Jim serving as Blaine County Treasurer in later years. Charlie Russell was a close personal friend of the McCoy family and stayed at their home in Chinook on numerous occasions.

Jim McCoy was nearly eighty years old when he rode over the "Great Divide" in 1943 and was a true cowboy to the end, being horseback until shortly before his death. His pistol, gun belt and many personal effects are on display at the Blaine County Museum in Chinook. Unfortunately, a ton of good stories died with him.

Yeah, any shave tailed kid that wanted to be a cowboy could have learned a lot by visitin' with Jim McCoy.

100

Chapter Twenty

Wylie Coyote Finally Wins One

*W*e got caught in quite a snowstorm in the middle of October a few years ago. The calves were still on the cows out in the summer pasture, and we had a dickens of a time trying to get a little hay to them. We'd gotten over a foot of the white stuff with a nice stiff breeze, so even the four-wheel drive pickups full of hay didn't have a real easy time. As much as we can always use the moisture, I sure hope that doesn't happen again for a while. It turned way below zero too, so it sure knocked the dickens out of the calf weights that fall.

We didn't need to plow the critters out, thank Heavens, we just showed up with a pickup full of hay and a saddle horse, and they were sure ready for a fresh field; one with a little open water and maybe even a fork full of hay once in a while. The old girls were pretty glad to see us comin', I know that. We could pick around and find them a trail out of the coulees where the snow had blown off the ridges if we looked a while, and it sure didn't take long to trail them home once they got out on the county road.

That storm was pretty widespread, and the farther east you went the more intense it was. There were places in the Dakota's that got over two feet of the durn stuff, and they had cattle stranded everyplace. There were snowplows running around like crazy, trying to get the cattle closer to the haystacks.

A crisis in the West is where you can really tell what you're made of ... and what kind of neighbors you've got. Well, some of the folks in North Dakota were in a real mess, so the neighbors all got together to help each other out. One of them had a big four-wheel drive tractor with a dozer on it, so three or four outfits went together to help get everyone's cows home.

The Tolman's cattle were the last ones they got to, and it was getting pretty late in the day when they pulled into their field. There were several guys with horses, but even a horse had quite a time with that much snow on the level. The dozer went down the ridges, and a few at a time the boys broke a trail for them and got the cattle worked up to where they could follow the track that had been plowed.

Someone else had an outfit waiting in the trail with a few bales of hay, so there sure wasn't any danger of the cows scatterin' back out again. Keeping them from rubbin' the doors off the pickup was the biggest chore.

Those Dakota boys are fairly used to having a little winter, but this time it was a little tougher than even they were used to, and something happened that they hadn't seen before. As the boys on the horses were following the long line of cattle back home, they noticed three or four coyotes following in the trail behind them.

I guess the snow was even too deep for Dakota coyotes to travel, and that dozer trail looked like pretty good goin' to them, too. They were probably a little on the hungry side and hoping that the boys would have an old cripple that couldn't make it all the way home. "After all ... a coyote has to eat, too."

Coyotes can get pretty brave when they're in a bunch and about half starved, and these just kept getting closer and closer as the late afternoon started turning to evening. At long last they made the final turn into the Tolman's home field, with the coyotes still right on their tail ... trotting slowly up the trail behind them.

"I'm headin' to the house to get a gun," one of the guys yelled. "Those coyotes are just a little too bold for my likin'."

"I'll get 'em," young Billy Tolman answered, pulling a big Colt 45 revolver out from under his sheepskin coat.

"You can't hit nuthin' with that dang thing," his Dad hollered. It was too late, Billy had already wheeled his horse around in the narrow trail and was headed straight toward the pack of coyotes at a dead run.

This strange turn of events more than likely caught the coyotes a little off guard. After all, they'd been following the whole outfit for a couple of hours, and nothing like this had happened before. They scattered in every direction, leaving the good going of the plowed trail and bounding through the deep snow.

Billy took in after the biggest and closest one, his horse also leaving the trail and lunging through the

103

deep snow behind their intended victim. Getting a good pistol bead on a coyote from the back of a horse lunging through three foot snow banks is apparently not as easy as they make it look in the movies.

Oh, Billy's horse ran right up on him alright, but just as he squeezed off his first round the plan went sour ... really sour. The gelding's head came up as he lunged through yet another snow bank, causing Billy's shootin' arm to come down. The result was a perfect shot ... right between his horse's ears.

The whole outfit folded up like an accordion in the deep snow. The poor old gelding was deader 'n a door nail ... never knew what hit him, and Billy's marbles were pretty well mixed up for a while. It was a dang wonder the fall hadn't kill him, too. He didn't know what had happened either, until someone explained it to him. The pistol was lost someplace in all of that deep snow, and wasn't found until the next thaw.

But, they say, "It's an ill wind that blows no good." Those old coyotes would probably agree with that ... if they had the guts to come back for the fresh horse-meat. I know one thing for sure ...

I certainly wouldn't have wanted to be standin' in Billy's boots when his old man got a hold of him.

"Quick ... run, Mabel!! I hear those
coyotes comin' right now!"

Chapter
Twenty One

Sourdough Sally

*A*fter an unusually hectic morning, I had the rare opportunity to actually have a good fresh cup of coffee yesterday. It was around ten o'clock or so, and I'd just settled into my rockin' chair with the cup in my hand when the kitchen door flew open.

"Grandad! You gotta come right now! I need your help! Quick!"

It was Faith, our nine year old. She and her sister Sally had spent the previous night with us. Being fairly accustomed to the fact that their perception of immediate crisis and mine are not always on the same page, I wasn't unduly alarmed. After all, I hadn't even had one sip of that coffee yet.

"Oh, yea? So what's the big problem? Can't I finish my coffee first?"

"No! You gotta come right now! I roped that yearlin' colt down in the corral and I can't get the halter on him, and I don't want him to choke!"

"Well," I thought to myself. "Maybe this isn't just another one of her over-exaggerations. This DOES sound like sort of a crisis."

There are six or eight head of horses down in the corral, and I could just envision the yearlin' with a rope around his neck, all tangled up in the bunch, with hooves flying in all directions and my little nine year old cowgirl in the middle of the cyclone.

I don't think I ever did get that cup of coffee. I went right down to help untangle the mess. It wasn't quite as bad as I'd envisioned. She'd had the sense to get him in a pen by himself, so my fears of her getting tromped under by the other horses were unfounded. We finally got the halter on and tied him up in the barn. She's staked a claim to that colt and informed me she's going to start breakin' him.

"He'll be big enough to ride by next spring, won't he, Grandad?"

"Yea, he should be big enough by then," I answered. "But you can sure spend some time with him and get him gentled down between now and then."

Question? How many nine year old girls do you know would tie into a wild yearlin' colt with a rope ... and actually manage to catch him? Not too many, I suppose.

I don't think that little wild horse incident was just an accident. Something like that takes a lot of self confidence, and resourcefulness. Those are things that have to be taught and then hopefully learned through experience and encouragement.

I think that's the place where some of us older folks often drop the ball. It's ALWAYS easier and faster to just go do a job by ourselves than it is to include the kids, but taking the extra time to encourage and include the young 'ns always pays off in spades.

Some cattle needed a change of pasture earlier in the week, which is why we had three little girls camping here. We had to roundup and trail a bunch of cows about twelve miles to a new field. I've done that a lot of times by myself; just me horseback with a dog. As far as moving those cattle was concerned, I dang shore didn't need three little girls and their "help." But, when you stand back and look at the big picture, that's exactly what we needed.

Boy, were they excited. You'd o' thought we were trailin' cows all the way up here from Texas. To say the least, the logistics were a little complicated with all the extra cowgirls involved. Here was the crew: Faith, age nine, a dang good hand for her age and mounted well; Rio Dawn, eight years old, a city cousin, riding a two year old filly she'd been breaking that only had a couple of rides outside the corral; and Sally Anne, five years old. Sally was riding Benny, an old retired and ring-boned, twenty something year old geldin' that fit her perfectly.

We gave each of the gals a nick name on the way to the roundup, and Sourdough Sally was the tag we hung on the littlest gal. She's the one that probably got the most positive benefit from the day, and her reaction was well worth all the extra pain in the neck.

Sally has a speech impediment, and because folks have trouble understanding what she's trying to say, her self confidence really needed a shot in the arm. There have been a lot of times that I've seen her just hang her head and not answer when someone speaks to her because she knows they won't understand her anyway.

107

It was discovered not long ago that she's "tongue tied," and that's been her problem all along. Why in the world everyone (including the doctor and a year's worth of speech specialists) had failed to detect that before now seems amazing, but that was the case. The doctor fixed it recently and she's doing a lot better already.

Sally really didn't want to go. She hasn't ridden all that much, and was a little afraid. I really had to dig into my psychological bag of tricks to talk her into it, and I'm sure glad I did. Here are three methods I use on the kids regularly and the order I use them in:

1. Necessity; ("I <u>NEED</u> the help." Everyone likes to be needed and feel useful.)
2. Encouragement; ("You can ride that ol' horse. He doesn't buck very hard ...
   I <u>KNOW</u> you can do it.")

And as a last resort ...

3. Conscription; (Don't give the little yay-hoos any real choice.)

Soooo ... here we go ... crew and all. I had to ride Rio's two year old filly on the roundup to top her off so she could handle her, and Rio and Sally rode the old geldin' double. Faith was certainly hand enough to hold up her end of things, and it's just a matter of time until the other two do as well.

When we finally got strung out down the county road, Sally took over on her own horse, and rode for ten miles straight, only getting off once for a potty break. When we finally got the cattle where they needed to go, she didn't want to quit. She was so proud of herself that it made the whole ordeal worth the effort.

Sourdough Sally, Cowgirl

When we finally got back in about supper time, she marched into the kitchen with her chest poked out and triumphantly declared, "I did dood, Nana. Wee-wee dood. Ol' Benny neber eben bucked."

Take a little extra time for a kid or two. You'll be glad you did.

109

"Conscription! Did you hear that? Conscription!
No wonder they show up out here in the pasture
with all those kids and horses! Tell me, just
where's a gal like me supposed to hide?

I'm going to report that joker to PETY that's what
I'm going to do!"

Editor's Note:

PETY is an acronym for ...
People for the Ethical Treatment of Young 'ns

(A radical organization of people with no kids.)

Chapter Twenty Two

But Honey ... I Got Hung Up

$\mathcal{M}$y reputation has taken quite a hit after years of running all over the country to play my guitar while I leave my little honey home to do all the work. Actually, it's a pretty good arrangement from my perspective, and it's absolutely amazing what a dinky little ninety-five pound gal can get done when I'm not home to get in her way.

I've only had to call home for more money two or three times, but let me tell you what, those were not a pretty sight. I think the physical and mental retribution I experienced from those rare (but very painful) incidents would have easily fit into the spousal abuse category.

What I really need to figure out is an iron clad sort of an alibi to get me out of those jams that occasionally just reach out and grab me. You know ... sometimes stuff just happens, and I have to dream up a perfect excuse to drop on the boss that will somehow explain everything and get my foot out of the trap. What I need is a perfect line ... one like Larry Nissen has.

Larry's reputation is about in the same shape as mine. He's been known to take off right smack dab in the middle of calvin' and leave poor Patty home with all the chores to do. His excuse is even lamer than mine ... he sneaks off to play cards. But, he's pretty good at it, and I've heard rumors that he's got a bunch of those plastic ice cream buckets full of money buried all over the ranch.

As you can imagine, Patty hasn't been privy to EVERYTHING he does, but he's always had a standard line for being home late. "But Honey, I got hung up ... or I'd o' been home sooner." He usually drags in sometime AFTER the chores are all done.

I don't think Patty ever really believed him. That's got to be one of the lamest excuses I've ever heard, but he always seemed to pull it off, and somehow managed to miraculously get "un-hung" just as soon as all the chores were done.

And speakin' of miracles ... that Larry must have been born under a lucky star. His "Hung-Up" alibi got validated a year or two ago, and Patty's been believin' it ever since. Here's the scoop:

It was calvin' time at the Nissen Angus outfit and Larry went out before breakfast to let a baby calf in with a cow. It was one of those trade-a-calf graft jobs. Patty was in the house whippin' up some hotcakes. It wasn't supposed to take him very long ... it was just sort of routine. They'd been at it a couple of days, and the gentle old cow was pretty used to the drill.

The cow was in a pen at the barn, and a couple of times a day, Larry would get her a little bite of grain and let her out of the pen to follow him down the alleyway where he'd pour the grain in a pan by the head catch. The ol' girl would stick her head in the grain pan and catch herself while Larry let the hungry baby in to help himself to breakfast. It usually only took about ten minutes or so.

This particular morning, things didn't go at all according to the plan. Larry stopped to pick up the gallon of grain and let the cow out of the pen, just like he always did. She marched behind him down towards the head catch, just like a little soldier ... so far so good, but here's where the wicket gets a little sticky. When Larry bent over to pour the grain in the pan, the over exuberant Mama cow bumped him in the rear end in her haste to get to her breakfast, and knocked his clumsy frame forward. He fell face down into the grain pan.

"CLICK!"

Yea ... that's what happened alright. Larry's head AND the cow's head were firmly stuck in the super-duper, patented, never-slip head gate. Larry was on the bottom, and the cow's head was on top. She didn't even seem to mind the fact that he was slobberin' all over her grain ... she just ate around him, conscientiously licking off the rolled barley that had conveniently stuck to his balding head.

Meantime, back in the ranch house, the phone rang and Patty lost all track of time. Larry got in about forty-five minutes of quality head-catch time before she went out to the barn to see what was taking so long. As she pulled the lever to set them both free, his line was a classic ...

"Sorry about bein' late for breakfast ... but Honey,
I got hung up ... or I'd o' been home sooner."

It was perfect. She's been believin' him ever
since.

Chapter
Twenty Three

Don't Ask ... Don't Tell

"Doggone it, Marge ... how come those kids o' ours went 'n planned this big shindig anyway? You should o' headed this deal off," Tom grumped as they turned their car around in the ranch yard.

"Being married sixty years is a big milestone," Marge smiled with anticipation. "Besides, they just wanted to have a little get together to honor us, that's all. Don't you dare be an old grump. They've gone to a lot of work for all of this."

"This dang necktie is killin' me! You know how I hate these big spectacles ... reminds me of a funeral or somethin'. Where'd you say this was s'posed to be? Are we goin' to the Eagles, or the Elks or the Moose? I always get those places all mixed up ... I just know it was at one of those animal deals."

"It's at the Eagles Lodge ... and please slow down, we've got plenty of time to get there."

Reluctantly Tom slowed the car down. He was resigned to the fact he was going to have to go through with this, even though he was sure he was going to hate every minute of it. The kids meant well, he thought, even though he would have preferred they'd have forgotten the entire thing.

Marge, on the other hand was really looking forward to it, and wondering about things like the cake and the table decorations, and especially the program where some of their grandchildren were certain to do something fun.

The next few miles passed in silence as each of them reminisced the last sixty years in their minds; the good times and ... the not so good ones that had made up their life together. Tom finally broke the silence, his demeanor suddenly softer from the miles of memories.

"Yea, who would have thought we'd be sittin' here in this car on the way to our sixtieth anniversary party when we got married in 1946? Where has all the time gone? I just want you to know that you've been about the best wife a fella could have ever had," Tom said, making his usually gruff tone as soft as he could, "and when I promised you not to be unfaithful to you, that's just what I meant ... I never have."

"I know," Marge smiled lovingly from across the front seat.

There was suddenly a big question mark in Tom's mind that had never found its way there before. "You ever been unfaithful to me, Marge?"

After a very long and uncomfortable silence, he finally received the dreaded answer.

"To be perfectly honest, Tom ... yes, I have. Three times."

Tom was justifiably devastated by her response, and was now wishing he'd never asked. This certainly wasn't the reply he was expecting. Another mile or two of silence followed as he considered this new piece of unwanted information.

"When?" he finally gained the courage to ask.

Marge seemed lost in her thoughts, and at long last began to relate the bittersweet memories.

"Do you remember when we first bought the ranch and were droughted out and the banker called our loan? Then, do you recall how I mentioned to you that maybe if I talked to him he might change his mind?"

"Yer, kiddin'! I just thought it was a miracle ... that danged old skunk!" Tom's mind traveled back in time, and after a long time of reflection he finally responded. "Well, we WERE goin' to lose the whole outfit," he said dejectedly.

"And then there was the time you needed that heart surgery, and we didn't have any insurance ... remember? Well, if you'll recall I made a little visit to the doctor to "check on the details". Then, do you remember how he called the next day and said he'd decided to do the operation for free?"

"No ... really?? I jus' thought he needed a tax deduction or somethin'."

"Well," Tom continued after a long pause, "I guess it WAS a matter of life 'n death." As much as he was devastated by the news, he could distinctly see the faint trail of justification.

Another couple of miles of silence passed, as the old cowboy digested all of this new found information. They were nearly to the outskirts of town by the time he found the courage to ask the question burning in his mind.

"Didn't you say there were three times? What's the story on the third time?" he asked at long last, dreading the answer he'd receive.

"That one was about twenty years ago," Marge answered as gently as she could. "Do you remember the time you were running for President of the Stockgrower's and needed those extra 68 votes to win?"

"Yea, Dick ... It's jus' like I figgered.
When she comes to politics you better not trust
NOBODY."

Chapter Twenty Four

Uncle Muck's Banjo

This little story started back in the late 1800's sometime, and as incredible as all of this is going to sound, I'll swear on a stack of Bibles that it's 100% the truth. I'm going to have to give you a little background information to get you up to speed on this little deal, so bear with me.

I used to have an old Great Uncle that lived down in the Ozark Mountains of southern Missouri. His name was Melvin Reese, but everyone just called him "Muck". Exactly how he got that handle, I don't have a clue. It seems like all of those hillbilly relatives of mine have nicknames for some reason.

Because I was the oldest, smartest, and handsomest of all their grandchildren, my Grandad and Granny used to haul me all over the place on big road trips to visit our kin folks. Uncle Muck was always everyone's favorite. A tall, long-armed, red headed character with a contagious laugh, he was

119

Uncle Muck
Alias: Melvin Reese   circa 1990

always jokin' around about something. When he'd tell a story, he'd get so tickled at it himself that he'd have the entire room crackin' up just watching him laugh at his own story.

In true hillbilly style, Uncle Muck would rather hunt and fish than eat. He also played a mean five-string banjo, and I can just see him with his head reared back and his mouth wide open, belting out his famous Ozark rendition of "Cripple Creek". He was a real hero of mine.

On one occasion we were down in "Bugger County" in the Ozarks on a little visit, and I convinced Uncle Muck to get out his banjo. He did, and (again) I was totally enthralled. "Ah, I don't play it much anymore ... in fact I don't think I've picked 'er up since the last time you was here. ...got arthur-ite-us in m' fingers."

Bein' smart like I am, I picked up right away that a budding young musician such as myself (probably 8 or 9 years old ... without arthur-ite-us) could probably use a good banjo like that, and I spent the biggest part of the next couple of days trying to talk my favorite Uncle out of that good banjo of his. After all, he'd already said that he didn't play it much anymore.

Finally, probably out of desperation ... to get me to shut up, he told me that he just couldn't bear to part with that old banjo, but there was one up in the attic that I could have if I wanted it. "She might need a little fixin' up, though ... to make 'er work right."

Well, Uncle Muck could possibly have been the Ozark King of Understatement. The head was busted, the strings and tuning pegs were missing, and it had been played so much that there were holes in the neck where the favorite chords had been played for the last 75 years or so. It needed a "little fixin' up" all right.

Fast forward about 40 years or so now, and that old 1880's model relic was still hangin' on my wall. It really didn't take a genius like me all that long to figure out that the old thing was way too far gone to fix up. But it DID have character, and it WAS Uncle Muck's so it had earned its spot on the wall as a decoration. It brought back a lot of good ol' memories of the long ago days and that favorite old Uncle, now passed on to his Reward.

A travelin' band happened to be playing in town a few years ago, and because I knew some of them, they stopped out at our place for a visit before they headed back out on the road. One of the guys in the band was Jake Peters. Jake has been the Canadian Champion five string banjo picker so many times that he doesn't even enter the contests anymore. He just doesn't have any real competition.

Jake also builds and repairs instruments, and when he spied my old wall hanging, wanted to know the story behind it. I told him the tale, and he offered to take it back to Alberta with him and fix it all up as good as new. Because it was an old family heirloom, and it would be nice to see it play again, I agreed.

I got a call from my Canadian friend a year or so later, and he informed me that he'd found a banjo in a second hand store up north of Edmonton that was a dead ringer for Uncle Muck's, and he figured that there were parts enough to make one good one out of the two.

Well, that's just what he did. He had the metal parts re-plated and fixed the neck and tuning pegs as good as new. Although he'd been very careful to keep it entirely original, it probably looked even BETTER than it did when it was new.

"I never did find a maker's mark on it anywhere," Jake grinned proudly as he handed over Uncle Muck's pride and joy. It looked like it had just come out of a store window. "All I could see was a No. 25 written by hand on the inside of the wooden tone ring."

"Did you ever look on the old parts banjo?" I asked. "If you think they're made by the same guy, then maybe there's a mark on that one."

"Nope, I never did ... let's take a look."

We had to back out a couple of screws and slide the shiny metal ring off to get a look at the inside of the wooden ring. There it was ... for all the world to see ... in the same hand writing as on Uncle Muck's banjo ... No. 26!!

Here we had two banjos approximately 125 years old ... made by the same guy, that were only one number apart! One of them had spent most of its life in the Ozark Mountains and the other one had some-how wound up over 2000 miles away in Canada. It's hard to imagine that they had actually lain side by side on their maker's bench all those years before.

Fast forward with me once more ... another six or eight years or so. I happened to get an email from a lady I'd never met. She's a musician also, and was wondering if we were related. It turns out we are, as Uncle Muck was her Grandad. It's funny how families drift apart, isn't it? I just couldn't resist telling her the entire banjo story, and how incredible the consecutive numbers were.

She was moved to tears ... you see, her Mother had wound up with Uncle Muck's good banjo when he'd died, but it had been stolen out of their house one day while they were away. That had been several years ago now, and a thorough search of the pawn shops had turned up absolutely nothing. It appears that old banjo was lost forever ... memories and all.

Was it just a coincidence that Jake Peters found the parts banjo north of Edmonton with a consecutive number, at least 2000 miles away from its old partner? ... Maybe.

Was it purely accidental that a long lost cousin happened to contact me ... a guy she'd never met, and then was moved to tears when she heard a simple story about a dumb banjo? ... Perhaps.

Was it just a twist of fate that it happened to be the Christmas season ... the time of year when we think most about giving gifts and blessing others? I heard a guy say once that giving can't actually even be considered giving ... until we give up something we REALLY want to keep. Well, just by coincidence, I REALLY wanted to keep that banjo ... but, I also knew where it belonged.

There's one thing that I KNOW wasn't any coincidental accident. When my new-found cousin Jena got that surprise package with her Grandad's banjo in it just before Christmas that year ... she probably wet her pants.

124

Chapter Twenty Five

Billy 'n the Bull 'n the Biffy

"*I* don't care if we ain't got the mowin' machine quite ready to go, I think we oughta knock off 'n go to Warrick anyway," Dick snorted as he wiped his greasy hands on some tall grass. "Besides it won't take over a couple of hours to finish fixin' 'er. We can get it goin' in the mornin' when we get back home."

The boys had ALWAYS taken in the big Fourth of July rodeo in beautiful downtown Warrick, Montana, and had NEVER started haying until after the big holiday anyway, but this particular year back in the fifties their work was way behind. They actually had some meadows with hay tall enough to cut for a change, so they were both chompin' at the bit to get going.

"Yea ... in fact let's just knock off right now an' head on over there," Billy agreed. I hear that new school teacher is stayin' there this summer ... I might even ask 'er fer a dance."

"She wouldn't even look at an ugly ol' buzzard like you when she's got guys like me to pick from," Dick jeered as he dropped his tools on the ground and headed for the house.

Well, this just happened to be the Fourth of July, and although the boys had totally given up on the idea of going to the rodeo and the big dance this year, they'd somehow just managed to talk themselves back into it. Lots of buckin' horses, the promise of copious amounts of fermented liquid refreshments, and a pretty school teacher to dance with were just more of an attraction than they could resist. In two hours they had on their very best shirts and were rattlin' down the trail towards a big day of fun.

The big Fourth of July rodeo in Warrick is just history now, but it was quite a blowout back then. They were late, so hadn't even bothered hookin' up the trailer and taking their horses, but they did throw in their bronc saddles just in case they got there in time to enter up.

They pulled into the rodeo grounds a little before noon, just as the entries were closing, and Billy signed up in both the saddle bronc and bareback ridin', and Dick got in the bronc ridin' and the bull doggin'.

It was a beautiful summer day and the place was packed. There were cars and people all over the hillsides with picnic lunches and kids running wild. Billy was still thinkin' about how he was going to get to meet that new school teacher, and kept cranin' his neck around to see if he could catch a glimpse of her. Of course all his gazing around at the crowd didn't go unnoticed, and Dick just kept jobbin' him.

"If that gal is smart enough to teach school, she's bright nuf not to talk to a guy with a face like a used saddle bag ... 'specially one like you that ain't got

126

any money," he teased. "You'd flat have to have 'er cornered 'fore she'd even give you the time o' day."

"Oh yea? I'll show you a thing 'er two about wimmin if you got brains enough to figger it out," Billy retorted.

Actually, if the truth were known, Billy was about as bashful as they come, and by the time he'd ingested enough liquid courage to actually try to strike up a conversation with a gal, he was in bad enough shape that no decent lady would have anything to do with him.

Before long the rodeo was underway, and Billy's bareback ride went pretty good. He wound up in second money. Dick drew a big black Percheron mare that bucked him off in about four jumps, and his "partner" was really giving him the dickens.

"Guess I'm gonna have to give you ridin' lessons AND girlin' lessons ... my Gramma can ride that good."

Dick just glared.

"Don't need no lessons from the likes o' you ... but I AM thirsty." Dick headed up the hill where the beer truck was parked and doing a land office business.

"Hey ... wait fer me," Billy stumbled to catch up.

Meanwhile back at the rodeo arena, one of the neighbors had brought over a big ornery Charolais bull to see if he would buck, and they ran him in behind the saddle broncs. Some kid from Rocky Boy had volunteered to get on him for an exhibition ride. I'm not really sure what happened next, but the bull bucked the ol' kid off and was really on the fight, chargin' everything in sight.

The team ropers were just getting ready for their chance to participate, and unfortunately the sleepy head that was running the gate to let them into the arena had his back turned. The deranged bull bumped through the half open gate with blood in his eye, and the first thing he saw was Billy; just stumblin' along there minding his own business, headed for the beer truck.

The crowd shrieked and Dick and Billy both turned around to see Mr. Bull with the seat of Billy's pants in his sights. Dick was ahead enough to be out of the path of destruction and let out a yell at his partner. Billy was instantly motivated to move quite a little faster than is his custom. I mean to tell you, that boy can run when he's scared.

The first place the would-be victim could see to escape was the biffy, a full hundred and fifty feet away. Taking at least 15 foot strides, Billy was there in no time, with the bull hot on his rear. He nearly jerked the door off its hinges and slammed it behind him, leaving the bull skidding to a stop. Mr. Charolais knew he was in there and was causing an awful ruckus; bellerin', shaking his head, pawing up the dirt, and blowin' his nose on everything for fifty feet.

Just when Dick was sure Billy had made it to safety, the biffy door flew open and Billy tore back out of there, trying to make a run for it. Nothin' doin' … the bull ran him right back in there again. This little trick was repeated three or four times, with Billy coming back out and the bull running him right back in.

Finally the pickup men came to the rescue and got a rope or two on the bull, and Billy made a run up the hill where Dick had been watching the fun from on top of the beer truck.

"Dang fool … why didn't ya just stay in there?" Dick snorted.

Billy didn't even answer. He just stared down at his boots, trying to catch his breath. When the biffy door finally opened again, Dick at last figured out Billy's predicament. The pretty young school teacher emerged, straightening her clothes and her hair, with a face nearly as red as Billy's.

Dick couldn't help joshin' just a little more. "Well, did you ask her t' the dance while ya had 'er cornered?"

"Fer Cryin' out loud, Billy ... Ya HAD 'er
cornered! If ya want a gal t' dance with ya
... ya gotta <u>ASK</u> er."

Chapter
Twenty Six

Basquin' In Profits

There was an eagle out in our calving pasture this morning. The doggone thing was just standin' there flat footed, and must have been at least four feet tall. It sort of surprised me, as we see them flying around or perched up in a tree quite often, especially this time of year, but this is the first time I've come across one just standing in the field. A cow had calved on that spot the night before, and I guess he was having a little breakfast on the placenta.

I think I must have been at least twenty years old before I saw an eagle around here. They're pretty common now that their populations have improved, but there just weren't any in these parts years ago. So far they haven't been a problem, but seeing him this morning reminded me of a story I heard about an encounter one of the stately old birds had with and elderly Basque sheep man a few years ago.

I guess his given Basque name was Pascal Alègre, but all anyone ever called him was Pete. He'd come to America as a young man from his homeland in the Pyrenees Mountains. Basques are a pretty unique bunch of people. They live in an area right on the border between France and Spain that is claimed by both countries. Funny thing though ... they really aren't French or Spanish or even a mixture thereof. Their language is completely distinctive too, and is totally unrelated to any of the other European dialects. Basque ancestry is really a mystery to historians and the best they can do is sort of guess how all of that came about.

Pete was sixteen when he landed in southern Idaho in the early 1930's. The only two words of English he knew were "hi" and "thanks", but he had a cousin in the sheep business and landed a job as a herder on the high desert. It was a perfect arrangement. Pete, like most of his countrymen, really knew his sheep and the woolies didn't seem to mind at all that he spoke to them in his native tongue.

The thirties were tough. There just wasn't any money. Of course, Pete wasn't used to having much anyway, so he hardly noticed. Instead of cash, he just took his herder's wages in lambs. By the time the Second World War broke out he had an entire band of 1500 head of ewes free and clear, and so he struck out on his own.

Pete was a frugal guy and a good operator. Some say he was just plain tight with a dollar, but his lamb crop was always one of the best to hit the market every year. Time passed and Pete and his family prospered even more. By the 1960's they had a very substantial ranch, stocked with the best Marino sheep that money could buy.

132

Unfortunately, a few years ago some of the neighborhood eagles developed a taste for those good Marino lambs. The modus operande of an eagle in a herd of sheep is to swoop down and snatch a lamb, then carry it to a nice high altitude and cruelly drop it to its death before having lunch on its little wooly carcass.

Pete was not impressed. Eagles are protected, you know. Endangered species, they say. That may be true, but it never was more true of any bird than one caught within ten miles of one of Pete's sheep. They were REALLY endangered if Pete could get a bead on one of them.

The Government has hunters for that sort of thing, so being the law abiding type, Pete called Max the local guy in charge of predator control, to come out and take care of things. They were both in Pete's floppy fendered old Ford pickup, bouncing out across the prairie to view the site of the last victim of an eagle killing. Max was pretty green at this sort of thing, not having encountered problems with eagles before. To say the least he was a little skeptical.

"Dare's eagles been packin' off m' lambs," Pete explained in his broken English. "Jush dive down 'n git 'em."

Max still didn't believe it, and was trying to figure out exactly what was REALLY happening. Just then out of the azure blue sky, a dive bombin' Bald Eagle came nearly straight down, snatching a bleating lamb from right in front of the old pickup.

"&^%*$#!"

I'm not sure what that Basque word meant, but I doubt very much if it was at all complimentary to Mr. Eagle. As the big bird and his lamb chop lunch slowly began to gain altitude, Pete screeched to a halt and pulled a rifle from behind the seat, taking aim at their uninvited dinner guest. Max was appalled.

KERPOW ...

"You can't kill that eagle! There's a ten thousand dollar fine for killing an eagle!"

"Meebe I can't ... KERPOW ... but he's got m' lamb ... KERPOW ... KERPOW ... don't worry doe ... KERPOW ... I got m' checkbook."

"No ... I'm <u>NOT</u> just another pretty face.
I can <u>SING</u> too!"

Chapter Twenty Seven

Cowboy Pride

Cowboys as a rule are sort of an independent bunch. Whether they're ridin' for someone else's brand or their own, they like to do their own thinkin' as much as it's possible, and generally won't stand for all that much foolishness. Consequently, those that ride for other folks will just move on rather than put up with what they consider "operational stupidity," and those that have their own outfit tend to march to their own drummer, and "the heck with the way anyone else does things."

The work-a-day cowboys have to put up with the boss ... sometimes a trust funder that's not even half the hand they are ... boy, that would be a tough one ... and most of the guys that have their own outfit have to deal with a banker that doesn't know which end of a cow to put the hay in. Life for a cowboy can be a challenge, can't it?

I've been giving this mindset a little thought lately, and I think it has to do with a generous dose of the sometimes fatal "cowboy pride." Pride in what you can get done well is a good thing in general, but it sometimes gets a little out of hand. For instance, asking for help in a tight spot is the absolute LAST resort. It's viewed as an admission of failure.

If a fella has to ask for a hand to get himself out of a jam, then in his mind, just maybe he isn't cowboy enough for that particular job. Now, that's humiliating. It really doesn't matter if it involves a horse and a rope or a check book and a ranch budget; we all tend to want to prove to the world that we can "git 'er done" on our own.

Although it's entirely possible that this could be a serious genetic defect when it's carried to extremes by the boots and hat crowd, I'm a firm believer that the rest of the world would benefit from a healthy dose of it. A little more pride in self accomplishment would do a lot of good for this old country. It seems to me that most everybody has their hand out nowadays, and there's no pride left.

Lonnie Mathews was one of those guys that took this entire concept to extremes. He was a heck of a hand, but would be offended if anyone offered him any help; no matter how tough his situation looked to the rest of us. He was as good a hand with a horse as you'd ever find, and was always schoolin' a spoiled one that someone else couldn't handle, or had already messed up.

On one occasion, he was riding a big bay thoroughbred he'd gotten from a lady that had spoiled him absolutely rotten. I think he just lived for the challenge some of these hopeless projects presented. Most guys would never mess with something like that. This ol' pony was a nine or ten year old gelding, right at sixteen hands high, and pretty as a picture, but had been given his own way so long that taking orders from a lowly cowboy just wasn't on his agenda.

Lonnie named his new horse Spunky. I think it pretty well fit, but if he'd been my project I think maybe his name would have had a couple more unrepeatable adjectives on the front of it. He was a terrible son-of-a-gun. Spunky really wasn't that bad to buck, but gettin' on him was a REAL challenge. He'd reach up with a hind foot and kick the stirrup so hard that it would ring like a bell, and wouldn't let poor ol' Lonnie even close to him.

We knew better than to offer any help, and were wondering how in the dickens this was all going to turn out. One particular mornin', Lonnie got him saddled and in the trailer OK, but when we got to the lease to mount up, that's where the rub came. Ol' Spunky would let a fella up around his head, (as long as you had an oat bucket in your hand), but as soon as you moved around to get on ... WHAP! ... that hind foot would take deadly aim on the stirrup.

The rest of us were all mounted up and waitin', as Lonnie tried him a time or two with no luck. It didn't take a rocket scientist to figure out that he needed to go to plan B, (whatever that was) but we still knew better than to offer any help. Lonnie reached behind the seat in the pickup and came back out with a gunny sack and slipped it under the sides of the headstall on the bridle and up over ol' Spunky's eyes. He stepped right up in the saddle ... before that spoiled jug head even knew what happened.

After he got a good seat, Lonnie just reached up and jerked the blindfold off and stuck it in his coat for the next time he needed to mount up. We got strung out on our circle just fine, and although the bay was pretty inclined to stampede if he got half a chance, the rest of the day really went pretty well.

We'd ridden fairly hard for three or four hours, and met on the top of a big cut bank overlooking a chunk of country we hadn't covered yet and stopped to give our ponies a breather. After all those miles, Spunky wasn't near as feisty as he had been at daylight, and acted plumb broke. The spot where we'd stopped to rest looked like a classic buffalo jump. There was a little dry stream bed fifty or sixty feet below us with the cut bank itself being of gen-u-ine gumbo and nearly straight up and down. The only vegetation on it at all was a little hardy sagebrush scattered randomly across its face.

There were three or four of us there soakin' up the sun and gazing over the country we had yet to ride. A couple of the guys lit up smokes, and Lonnie (being the traditionalist that he is) began to roll one from the Prince Albert can he always had in his shirt pocket. The warm mornin' sun was nearly perfect, and the horses were enjoying the rest as much as we were. Their eyes were about half shut, with their ears flopping lazily off on each side.

As Lonnie scratched one of those old wooded farmer matches on his saddle to light his brand new roll-yer-own, things took a sudden turn towards the south. That dang match made a loud pop, as those old things sometimes do, and Spunky went from dead asleep to fifty miles and hour in one jump. The real problem was that he jumped straight off that cut bank and into the wide open spaces. It was at least fifty feet down to the dry sandy creek bed.

Those kinds of wrecks just sneak up on you, and happen before you even know it. We were almost afraid to look over the bank to see what we were sure would be the dead body of our partner and that jug head horse he was riding. Sure enough, there was the bay gelding layin' at the bottom with his head turned back under himself, looking for all the world to be as dead as a mackerel.

We figured Lonnie must be underneath him. At first we couldn't see hide nor hair of him, but I'll be doggoned if he wasn't about halfway down, desperately hangin' on to a piece of sagebrush with his left hand and his boots danglin' off into space. His freshly rolled cigarette was still clinched between his teeth, and his right hand had a firm hold on that defunct match.

In all the excitement, we temporarily forgot that Lonnie liked to do things on his own and didn't like folks to offer any help.

"You OK? Need any help?"

Our old partner was just as startled by the turn of events as we were, and didn't answer right away. Finally his reply came driftin' back up the cut bank.

"Yea, I guess I could use a little help. Can you get me another match? This one blew out, an' I got my hands full."

Spunky wasn't dead. We went down to assess the damage and were surprised to find he was still breathin'. That sandy creek bed has apparently softened the fall. We straightened his head out and he just laid there battin' his eyes for a minute or two, and then I'll be doggoned if he didn't stand up. He just stood there quiverin' with his legs all sprattled out for a while, but other than being kind of shook up that jug head was just fine.

Funny thing though ... he was easy as pie to get on after that. ➤

"Now, I'll tell you what, Dick. That pride is
bad stuff. That's why I made up m' mind
a long time ago not t' have any."

Chapter
Twenty Eight

Mac's Country Grit

*T*here are a lot of laws that get passed at all levels of government for the most honorable of reasons, but the results are just a disaster. I'm of the mind that the guys we send to Congress and the State Legislature to represent us, feel a deep inner need to DO something, so they pass more dumb laws. I think requiring them to remove an old law and taking it completely off the books ought to be mandatory before we allow them enact a new one. At least that way we'd have a better chance at breakin' even.

Here's a good case in point: I've got a grandson that lives in town, and not long ago he walked up and down the streets lookin' for work, and couldn't find any. Nope, it wasn't because there wasn't anyone that could use a hand. It's because he's fifteen years old, and you can't legally hire anyone until they're sixteen. Now, if that ain't the dumbest law I've ever heard of, it's got to be close.

141

If a kid doesn't know how to work by the time they get that age, it's already too dang late. Teachin' a kid what sweat tastes like won't hurt them a bit. Besides, it gives a young fella a real sense of pride to figure out that he's actually doing a man's work and pulling his own weight. We gave him a job (probably a better idea anyway), so he comes out to help us with the cattle after school. I know I'm probably violating some dumb law here; so just go get your handcuffs and come and get me.

We've got another little eight year old granddaughter that's had the opportunity to live in the country. She's really been my shadow for the last few years, and a week or so ago, she and I rounded up a pretty good sized bunch of cows on horseback and then spent a couple hours sorting them in the alleyway, with her as the gateman. She did a GREAT job, and I really bragged her up as we were coming in for dinner.

"Grandad, I don't FEEL eight years old."

"You don't act eight years old either, Faith. You act more like you're sixteen. You make your Grandad proud."

I'm convinced that's one of the greatest assets of growing up in rural America; learning responsibility and the pride of self accomplishment at an early age. It literally pays dividends for a lifetime.

My friend Mac got started workin' when he was six years old. We always had more work than we could get done at home, so I didn't work out very much as a kid, but Mac's folks farmed him out to the neighbors. His first job was as a kitchen boy for one of the neighboring ranches, helping to feed the big haying crew.

He came from a big Irish family, and it didn't take long for folks to figure out that, "those McHenry kids really know how to work," so when anyone needed a hand, they came over to get one of them. Later, when he was in the sixth grade, Mac hired on to milk thirty head of cows after school, and then again before he caught the bus in the morning. He got five dollars a week and his room and board; not bad money for a kid with no expenses. It was five bucks more than he had before.

So, it was with this "nose to the grindstone" background that he worked his way through higher education and soon found himself a fresh graduate of a Veterinary Technical School. He landed a dream job for his required internship ... at the Dallas Zoo.

Things at the Zoo were always interesting. Mac was the direct assistant to the Head Veterinarian, and had all of the usual problems to deal with. There were the elephants with runny noses, and the giraffes with kinked necks, that sort of thing. He was having a ball; that was until he got called into the boss's office one day.

"Mac, I need for you to get some cotton swabs and sterile vials and collect some oral samples. We've got several of the snakes in the reptile garden that have some kind of an infection in their mouths, and we need to identify the source of the infection so that we can administer the proper medication to get it under control. I've seen something like this once before, and if we don't get a handle on it early, it could possibly become pandemic. If that infection begins to travel through the rest of their body, well ..." the old Veterinarian just slowly shook his head as his voice trailed off. "We've got some very valuable reptiles there, and we just can't take any chances."

Personally, I think I would have quit on the spot ... but not Mac. A crisis to one fella isn't necessarily an emergency from someone else's perspective. A snake with chapped lips isn't really all that high on my priority list. I'm not exactly sure if it was from stubbornness, pride in doing his job well, or just plain stupidity, but something in his Irish nature took control, and down to the reptile garden he went with his little doctor bag full of goodies.

Mac's very first patient was a big Diamond Back rattler about six feet long and nearly as big around as a stove pipe. He had two little beady eyes and a bad attitude, but sure as the world, there WAS a sore on his mouth, that was plain as day. Exactly how my stubborn Irish pal got that ol' Diamond Back's lips and the inside of his mouth swabbed for samples, I don't know ... but that was just the first one. They seemed to just keep finding more snakes that needed a sample taken.

Somehow the fresh new Vet Tech that had been given the opportunity to learn responsibility, ingenuity, and the value of a job well done as a kid, got it done. Mac returned to the office with all the samples he'd been sent for ... without gettin' bit even once.

I can understand from the Veterinarian's perspective, he would want to prevent the infection from spreading to the rest of the reptile's body. That would be very important, but I honestly believe I could have prevented further contamination a whole lot easier than having to endure Mac's blasted sample collection procedure.

I'd have just used a shovel ... and cut that infection off ... right behind his ears.

Chapter
Twenty Nine

Just Tryin' To Keep Warm

"*Holy* cow!" Billy grumbled as the wind blew the front door shut and he stomped the snow off his boots. "It must be a hun'erd below zero out there. I'd sure like to know where in the dickens all that global warmin' is that they been crowin' about."

"Must be BS. Get the feed pickup goin'?" Dick inquired as he flipped the hotcakes bubblin' on the stove. Daylight was just beginning to crack in the east.

"Yea ... she started, but just barely. Dang good thing we had 'er plugged in. Wish we'd a taken time to fix that doggone heater. It's gonna be a dang cold job without it. A fella could freeze plumb to death out there."

After a couple of unusually long pulls off the bottle of snake bite medicine they keep under the sink, the boys sat down to their breakfast, with Billy actually forgoing his usual fare of a totally liquid cuisine, and tying into the flapjacks like he was hungry. Cold weather always seems to be good for the appetite. (Here's the philosophy around that camp: A fella ALWAYS needs to have plenty of snake bite medicine handy ... AND it's also useful to keep a snake in your pocket ... just in case.)

"I guess maybe I'll work on the frozen water tank down by the barn if you want to do the feedin' this mornin'," Dick offered. "Pass the hotcakes, would ja?"

He flipped one off the top of the pile over to Ol' Lucky, who was layin' on the rug by the door. The pooch caught it in mid air and dispatched it in one gulp, with his gaze never leaving the table. He sure didn't want to miss the next one, and was never sure when one of the boys would sail one his direction. Their old shack never did heat up very well in cold weather, even though the stove pipe was glowing red in the dim light of the kitchen.

"If I wuz you, I think I'd get that propane heater out of the barn. You can set the bottle on the floorboard an' put the burner up in the seat. That oughta help some."

"Might work ..." Billy slowly digested the suggestion. "... but don't them things need air to burn? I sure don't want t' run out o' oxygen an' smother-cate in that outfit."

Dick just laughed. "Oh, I think there'll be air enough, all right. You musta forgot that there ain't been a window in the driver's door of that outfit since the 80's when you busted it out with the post maul."

146

"Yea ... guess I forgot," Billy returned with a sheepish grin. He tossed another hotcake over his shoulder, and again Lucky caught it in mid air.

With breakfast behind them, the boys straightened up the kitchen a little and then began pulling on layer after layer of winter clothes. Lucky gratefully gulped down the extra plate of pancakes that had been made just for him, and all three of them trudged out into the raw north wind to meet the day.

Billy took the advice and got the propane heater out of the barn, while Dick slogged off through the snow with a couple jugs of hot water to work on the frozen water tank. The propane bottle fit on the floor board of the pickup OK, and he propped the burner up on the seat, steadying it with part of the two weeks worth of used baler twine piled up on the passenger side. He got it lit right up, and it did make quite a difference. Even set at the lowest level, it put out a lot of heat.

Finally, he was ready to go. Lucky dutifully jumped into the back and they rattled and squeaked their way out to the hay corral. The first couple of loads things went just fine ... it was on the third trip that stuff really went haywire.

Billy was just finishing pulling the strings off the last round bale, when Lucky just couldn't control himself any longer. He couldn't stand for those cows to be eatin' that hay before it was unrolled, so he took a big bite out of a handy hind leg. The old bag let out a beller and flipped around to face her attacker, and a half a dozen others came to her rescue, all bawling

147

like banshees. Billy was sure he'd be tromped under in the ensuing battle, so he hollered at his pal to knock it off.

"LUCKY! ... Get in the pickup!"

So ... remembering that big plate of hotcakes ... the faithful pooch dutifully obeyed. Instead of holding his ground as he usually did, he turned on his heel and flew into the open driver's door of the pickup with a half a dozen cows hot on his tail. Unfortunately, unbeknownst to Lucky, someone had re-arranged the furniture in the pickup and his exuberant entry knocked over the heater, which fell into the two week's worth of strings, which in turn instantly caught fire.

Oh, boy. Billy's mornin' got a little busy there for the next few minutes. The only thing he had to put out a fire was his old scotch cap, which considering the size of the pile of fuel seemed a little inadequate.

If the passenger door would have opened, things might have gone a little better, but it's been stuck shut for a couple of years. After what seemed like a lifetime of beatin' on the flames and throwin' out strings, he finally got the propane shut off and most of the fire outside the cab, where they just let the rest of the strings burn on the snow.

The feedin' crew at long last limped back into the yard and re-tied their outfit up to the light pole with the extension cord. Dick had finished thawing out the water tank, and was busy stokin' up the wood stove as they came in the door. The earflaps were plumb burned out of Billy's scotch cap, the right arm was burned off of his coat, and both he and Lucky still had hair that was smokin'.

"Yea ... I think there's enough air all right," Billy offered as he pulled the cork and drained the snake bite medicine. "... seems like she burns just fine."

"Yea ... seems like she burns just fine."

"Can you believe the government actually
allows people of that intelligence level
to be in charge of <u>US</u>??"

"It's <u>NOT</u> right I tell you!
It's just <u>NOT</u> right!"

Chapter Thirty

The Blind Jockey & The Horse That Couldn't See

*L*ife holds a few advantages for being a little on the small statured side. Not too many mind you, but there are a few. I'm actually the big one in my family, but as a kid I could fit between any of the poles on the corral fence I could get my head through. Consequently, I had an avenue of escape from whatever critter was putting the run on us that some of the fat boys didn't have. Now that's handy. A fella doesn't have to run so fast if you know the guy with you won't fit through the crack in the fence.

You'll notice that a lot of pretty good saddle bronc riders are fairly small guys. There are some big guys that can get the job done well too, but by and large most of the good ones aren't all that huge.

I think Larry Kane was the best bronc rider I've ever known, and he was no bigger than a minute. He didn't weigh much over a hundred pounds, but boy could that guy ride. He was the RCA (that was before they changed the name to PRCA) Rookie of the Year back in the early '60s sometime and I've always maintained he could have been a world champion anytime he wanted to be ... he just didn't like the lifestyle well enough to pursue that gold buckle.

Unfortunately, there's more to that bronc ridin' stuff than just being the "right size." I think maybe having some talent might have a little something to do with it. It never seemed to help me all that much, but my brother John has always been the smallest of us boys and he was also (maybe just by coincidence) the best rider of the bunch.

John didn't ever ride many saddle broncs, except when we bucked out the work horses at home. In fact, about the only rodeoing John did was in high school, and then his specialty was mostly bull ridin'. (Practice from ridin' the neighbor's cows.)

There's an old sayin': "When the world serves you lemons; make lemonade." With John barely topping the hundred pound mark, he wisely decided that a bulldoggin' career might be a tough row to hoe, so as a young fella he left home for the racetracks. You don't see a lot of fat jockeys.

I'm not sure how he got started riding racehorses, but being a good rider and a real light-weight, it was just a natural choice for him. I think some of the racehorse people looked him up to exercise their horses and it was only a matter of time 'til they had him in silks and on the track.

It was kind of an exciting life for a young guy. He's got a ton of stories to tell and a scrapbook full of win pictures. Besides racing all over Montana, John rode a lot in western Canada in the summers then hit the trail to Phoenix and over into California in the winter.

Riding a winning racehorse is a real thrill. The only time I remember Jockey John saying he enjoyed not being in first place was when his horse was following one of the lady jockeys. Perhaps we shouldn't elaborate on that here.

Of course the owners all knew how their horses ran, and were full of advice and instructions about how to run each race, depending on the length of the race and the other horses in the field. One rainy summer day John found himself on the Canadian circuit, and the track in Saskatoon was a real mess. It had been raining for several days and the racetrack was the consistency of chunky tomato soup.

He was up on a bay horse named Jungle Fox, and the owner told him that the only way to ride that horse was to lead the pack.

"He's never won a race by coming from behind, John. Put him in the lead and keep him there."

Now, that sounds like good advice to me. I think that little piece of information will win just about any race. He only had one itty-bitty problem. Apparently ol' Jungle Fox didn't like the slimy track. As they came out of the starting gate, they were running dead last, and despite John's most valiant efforts, he just couldn't get any more out of him. If you've never been on a race track at the back of the pack when the mud is ankle deep, then you'll have to rely on your imagination to appreciate the amount of guck and mud that was flying their way.

Jockeys wear several sets of goggles on a track like that, one right on top of the other, and are constantly pulling the muddy ones down so they can see. Unfortunately, Jockey John had gone through all his goggles barely halfway through the race and was running completely blind. He couldn't see a thing.

153

Not wanting to crash into another horse, our little hero urged the big bay to the outside. There's usually a lot less traffic out there, so just hoping and praying there wasn't anyone in the way, he turned ol' Jungle Fox loose.

"I was blind as a bat, but was thinkin' that if I could only get him out of the pack where he could see where he was going, I could just let him go on his own."

When they crossed the finish line, Jungle Fox and Jockey John were in the lead. It was only when they got to the winners circle, that John finally realized that the blinkers the horse was wearing were packed with mud and he couldn't see anything either. They won the race despite the fact that neither one of them could see a thing. The horse was trusting the man, and the man was trusting his horse. BOTH of them were running

Jockey John
(Looks like a fella getting his picture taken would clean up a little, doesn't it?)

154

blind, and NEITHER of them knew that his partner couldn't see.

Perhaps you know that a jockey is weighed saddle and all before AND after a race. After this one Jockey John weighed five pounds too much, and they had to hose him and the saddle off to get them back down to 115 where he was supposed to be.

John and Jungle Fox in the Winner's Circle.
August 5, 1980 at Marquis Downs, Saskatoon

I think there are a few valuable life lessons to be learned here:

1. When the track of life delivers you a face full of mud, that's not the time to quit ... that's the time pour to on the spurs.

2. At those times when the trail ahead of you gets hard to see, and you're in danger of losing your

way, it might be a good idea to trust someone else's judgment ... someone that has as much to lose (or gain) as you do.

3. Don't forget the famous last words of wisdom from Jungle Fox's owner. "That horse has never won a race coming from behind." Well, he sure did that one, but he couldn't see so he didn't KNOW he was behind. He THOUGHT he was winning, so he did. A big part of winnin' comes from not seeing yourself as a loser.

4. All that stuff we've heard about "The blind leading the blind," and how it's all foolishness is pure BS. Jockey John and Jungle Fox proved that. Sometimes, in spite of everything, if you give it all you've got, you wind up in the winner's circle.

John Overcast & Traffic Scope
Winner's Circle ~ Desert Downs ~ Phoenix, Arizona
January 7, 1981

Chapter
Thirty One

Strange Tracks & A Missing Calf

There was a chilly breeze blowing the morning that Herman bounced out across the frozen cow pies covering the feed ground to haul a couple of bales of hay to his calving cows. A light dusting of snow covered the frozen ground, but all in all, it wasn't a bad day for calving. At least at these temperatures the calves didn't have to lay in the wet slop like they do when the thermometer starts to rise enough to melt things.

At first, all appeared fine. There were a couple of new calves with their Mom's on guard, and both appeared to have sucked already. A quick check of the babies that had been born previously didn't turn up any problems right away, either.

"Those new bulls sure didn't hurt us any," he thought to himself, satisfied with the strong, long bodied calves kicking up their heels in the early morning sun.

It wasn't until after he'd unrolled the second round bale of hay, that Herman noticed a cow that couldn't seem to find her calf. She was bawling for her baby and taking a little sniff of every calf she walked past ... trying desperately to find him, but not having any luck.

"That's the old gal that calved down by the tree yesterday afternoon," he said under his breath. (Herman talks to himself a lot, now that he's getting a little older. His memory isn't quite as good as it used to be, either.) He drove down to where she'd calved the day before, with the lonesome Mama trotting behind him, but her missing baby wasn't anywhere to be found. A quick check of all the usual hiding places didn't turn up a thing. They had a real mystery on their hands.

It wasn't until then that he noticed the strange pickup tracks angling across the field. Closer inspection revealed a different tire tread than the knobby tires on his old feed outfit. He was pretty close to a main road, and Herman came to the only logical conclusion.

"Doggone it, somebody's picked up that old girl's calf ... sure as the world."

Most of the time when something like that happens, there isn't any evidence at all, and it would be just plain luck to ever find the calf again. This time it was different. On top of the tire tracks in the snow, Herman was lucky enough to find a tail light the thief had lost when he'd bounced across a ditch. With all this newly discovered evidence, he headed right back to the house to call the Sheriff's Office.

"Yes, Ma'am," he informed the dispatcher. "It looks like we've had a calf stolen." A deputy got on the line, and Herman gave him all of the details. "Maybe if you guys would keep your eye out for a Dodge pickup with a tail light missin' ... I found one in the field, and it sure looks like a Dodge light to me."

The deputy assured him they'd get the word out and do all that they could to try to find the thief. Herman went back outside to finish the chores, his usually sunny outlook on the moral condition of his fellow man shaken a bit by the morning's turn of events. Meanwhile, back on the feed ground, a lonely mother was still pining for her lost baby.

By midmorning the chores were done, and Herman jumped into his town pickup and headed to the coffee shop. He made a quick circle just to check for missing tail lights before he went in, but didn't find a thing out of order. He sat right down at one of the "farmer tables" and began to unwind the morning's tale of woe, making sure that everyone knew about the tail light lens he'd found.

"I just can't believe how low some folks'll stoop. That's pretty gutsy ... just to drive right in a fella's field and pick up a calf like that. They sure must be hard up for money, is all I can say."

"Well, those baby calves are bringing quite a bit at the sale barn," one of the neighbors chimed in, "an' tomorrow's a sale day. I'd go up there and take a look around if it was me." All of the experts at the table agreed, and so with the consensus being what it was, Herman was already making plans to take in the cattle auction the next day.

Just then the door opened and another neighbor that hadn't been privy to the morning's excitement walked in.

"Hey, Herman ... you're liable to get a ticket if the cops catch you with that tail light missin'." Herman's mouth dropped open, and as the snickers at the table grew louder, the rusty gears in his head slowly started grinding away. It was only then that he faintly recalled checking the cows late last night in his Dodge "town pickup."

The café door opened again. This time it was the Deputy Sheriff ... just out crushing crime. "Who belongs to that Dodge pickup out there with the tail light out?"

I already told you that Herman talks to himself a lot. Well, I think he's started doing it a lot more lately. If he'd only kept all of this to himself he wouldn't have had quite so much to live down. Visits to the coffee shop were pretty hard to take for a while.

Oh, by the way ... when he got back home there was a hungry baby calf wagging his tail as he hungrily nursed his Mama. Oh yea, she'd found him someplace.

"Now ain't that about the dumbest thing you ever heard?"

Chapter
Thirty Two

Dancin' With the Dirty Shame Girls

*D*iversification ... now, I'm convinced that's the key to a successful ranching operation. That old guitar in the closet is the best piece of ranchin' equipment I ever bought. Although I've somehow talked my way onto stages all over the West, my show biz career hit a real highlight a while back.

I've always had a secret dream to share the stage with some real live gen-u-ine dancin' girls, and by George I finally got 'er done. (Please don't tell my Mom that's been one of my goals ... I don't think she'd understand. I'm pretty sure Dad would, but it's probably best not to bring it up ... out of self preservation he'd almost certainly deny it.)

My dreams finally came true one night in Wolf Point, Montana. The Dirty Shame Girls from Scobey were in town, fish net stockin's and all. We were down at a Cowboy Hall of Fame get-together. I'm thinkin' those gals are really going to put Scobey, Montana on the map.

I wish I was a little better at puttin' words down on paper, because they looked and danced WAY better than I can ever describe here. Holy Cow ... they were dancin' in a line and kickin' over their heads with those little short dresses of theirs and the diamonds on their garters would put your eye out. (Nope, that's not what happened to mine ... my story isn't near that good.)

"Dirty Shame Belles"

"The only thing those gals need to really go places is a good manager," I thought to myself. "You know, someone to drive 'em around from town to town and take care of all the details ... like holdin' that shoe horn to help 'em into those tight little dresses."

Apparently they're as good at mind readin' as they are at kickin' over their head, because it seemed like they avoided me all night.

Then I got to thinkin' ... here I am at the very pinnacle of my singin' cowboy career; on stage with the best lookin', highest kickin' chorus line in the State of Montana ... and then I remembered that I'd run off and left my little wifey at home to calve the heifers and it was at least ten below zero. I got to feelin' a little guilty, you know what I mean? There are times when having a conscience comes in handy, but this dang shore wasn't one of them. It wrecked my whole night.

It isn't that I haven't worked hard to get my singin' cowboy career to this point, 'cause I sure have, but now that I've finally arrived, my thoughts reluctantly drifted back to that freezin' shed full of calving heifers and my little Carhartt darlin' ... wollerin' around in the manure.

Boy, how I tried to get that picture out of my mind. I had plenty of mental images kickin' high right in front of me, without something like that sneakin' in the back door of my brain, but for some reason I just couldn't seem to shake it.

So ... out of gratitude, just to show my little sweetie how much I appreciated her, when I got back home I spent more money on her Valentine's present that year than I ever have. You should have seen it ... it was perfect. I got her a perfectly color coordinated red steel post driver to go with a pair of brand spankin' new matching red handled fencing pliers. (You know how sensitive those girls are about colors.)

I REALLY must have surprised her, because she was absolutely speechless. In fact while I was telling her all about the chorus girls, she didn't say a word the entire time.

She just kept staring at her new gift. I told her that I was really thinking about her 95 pound muscle mass when I picked out the thirty pound driver, because it took a lot less down pressure when she was driving those steel posts in the frozen ground. Again, she was so astounded at my extra thoughtfulness that she just looked at me in amazement, and didn't say a word.

It's no wonder everyone calls her Mrs. Lucky. Some gals can't even imagine what it would be like to have a loving and considerate fella like me around ever' day just showering 'em with presents. It's been a couple of days now since I gave her that special gift, and she's still speechless. In fact I don't think she's said three words to me since.

I had an awful bad dream last night. I don't remember what it was; I just remember that it was bad. I didn't wake up this morning until the sun was already way up in the sky, and I've got a terrible headache for some reason. I think it might have something to do with the big knot on my head just above my right ear. I don't have any idea where that knot came from, but for some reason Mama's new post driver is on the floor right beside the bed.

Doggone it ... I can't seem to find her around here anyplace. I s'pose she's probably just down checkin' the heifers.

Funny thing though ... all her clothes are gone.

Chapter

Thirty Three

No Peakin'

$\mathcal{O}$ccasionally folks will suggest that maybe I should consider gettin' a glass eye. To be perfectly honest, that never did make much sense to me. I've never run across one of those things that a guy could see out of anyway. Oh, there are times when they'd probably come in handy, but I think the bad out-weighs the good.

Several glass eye stories come to mind, as I give this a little thought. A friend of mine took her Dad's glass eye to school for "show and tell" when she was a kid. She thought that was pretty neat. After all, how many of the other kids had a Dad that kept an extra eye in the dresser drawer? If I remember right, I don't think Dad was very impressed.

There was a guy that used to work the ranches up this way a few years ago that had one. It kept gettin' him in trouble. As is the tendency of some of the less skilled ranch hands, he had a habit of hanging out in the skid row bars when he was in town. Now, that's enough to get a fella in trouble all by itself, but that glass eye sure didn't help any. I guess you sort of need to keep 'em greased up or they get stuck and won't track with the other one, and that tended to be a problem.

Well, this particular guy wasn't know for being all that fastidious with his personal grooming after he'd been in town for a few days, and that add-on eyeball of his had a habit of gettin' stuck looking off to one side or the other. "Off towards Jones's," is the way my Granny used to put it.

He'd be threading his way through the drunks just minding his own business, and unbeknownst to him, he was giving everyone at the bar the "evil eye." On more than one occasion, there'd be a fist come from out of nowhere, knocking a perfectly innocent man with a stuck glass eye into the middle of next week; and all because some guy didn't like the way he was looking at him. (The terms perfect and innocent might be a bit of a stretch, but this time he DIDN'T have it comin'.)

No thanks. I think I've got troubles enough without that.

Then there's the story of the old rancher down by Roundup. This was years ago and he'd hired a bunch of hillbillies that fell off a freight train to build some corrals for him. (As a side note, the term hillbilly is no longer politically correct, which is probably why I still use it. According to the social engineers, they should now be referred to as "Ozark Americans.") But ... I digress ... sorry.

These mountain boys were good workers as long as the boss was around, but as soon as he left they'd all sit down and quit diggin' post holes. Not only did they not know the boss had a glass eye, but their backwoods background made them ignorant of the fact that such a thing even existed. That all worked in the boss's favor one day when he needed to run into Billings for something. He just popped out his glass eye and sat it on top of a fence post.

"You boys just keep diggin' ... and no settin' down. You hear? Remember, I've got an eye on ya."

It worked like a charm. They were still sweatin' and diggin' several hours later when he came back to get his eye.

That little trick used to work for Sparky McCoy too, but the last time he tried it he wound up in the hospital. He was in a poker game in the back end of the Stockman Bar one night, and things were really going his way. Lady Luck was apparently sittin' right on his shoulder, and he'd accumulated a huge pile of chips on his side of the table.

"I gotta make a run to the john," he said as he popped out his glass eye and sat it beside his chip pile. "But don't worry; I'll be keepin' an eye on my stack."

Normally, that would be good for a laugh if nothing else, but this time things turned south. The cards had been dealt around while he'd been gone and his were laying next to his huge chip pile while the other players perused theirs.

One of the other guys in the game was an enormous greasy lookin' guy they called Sludge, who'd just blown into town with one of the oil rigs a week or two before. Nobody knew the new man very well, but it was fairly obvious that he wasn't the sharpest knife in the drawer.

Alcohol has been known to dim the wits of even the most brilliant of minds, and although Sludge definitely didn't fit into that category, he was doing his level best to mute what little intelligence he had. He'd had too much already, but ordered another tall one as Sparky returned to the table.

Being the evening's winner, Sparky was in an especially jovial mood.

"Luck ain't got nuthin' t' do with this game, boys," he joked. "She's all skill."

The rest of the players paid little attention to his baloney and had their eyes fixed intently upon the cards they'd been dealt. Just as Sparky took his seat, Maxine, the barmaid of more than ample frame, was delivering Sludge's eleven-teenth drink. The combined weight of the two oversized bodies on one side of the table was enough to sag the age-weakened floor of the Stockman just enough to send Sparky's glass eye casually rolling across the green felt table top.

No one paid any attention at first. They were all intent upon their cards. Well ... everyone except Sludge whose complete attention was firmly fixed on Maxine. She was obviously enjoying his admiring eyes, dimmed as they were.

As Maxine flounced back out of sight, Sludge dropped his eyes back to the cards in his hand. And there ... propped right against his skinny little pile of chips was Sparky's glass eye. Lookin' right up at his cards, too.

"I KNEW you was cheatin' all night!" Sludge thundered. "An' now yer lookin' at my cards!"

The following few moments weren't a pretty sight. The table, the cards, the chips, and Sparky's glass eye went flying through the air as the enraged bull of a man came after his pound of flesh. Sparky was out-gunned by at least 200 pounds.

He wound up in the hospital for two or three days, and didn't get his glass eye back for a couple of months. Someone finally found it under the juke-box.

Nosiree ... no glass eye for this cowboy. They're more trouble than they're worth. ▰

"So <u>THAT'S</u> the reason Sparky's always winnin'
them poker games. An' it's jus' too bad about
Sludge beatin' yer time with Maxine. Ever'body
knows them oilfield guys got more
money than cowboys ... even Maxine."

Chapter
Thirty Four

Observin' Tumbleweed Teddy

*W*ill Rogers must have been quite a guy. He had a few sayin's that are just as applicable today as they were when he first said them 80 or 90 years ago. Here's one of my favorites:

"There are three kinds of men: The ones that learn by reading; The few who learn by observation; The rest of them have to pee on the electric fence and find out for themselves."

Unfortunately, as I look over my shoulder, I think I've fallen into that last category a lot more times that I'd like to admit. I think it's probably some sort of a mental deficiency on my part, but then in this day and age of "victim mentality," just maybe I can figure out a way to blame all that stupidity on someone else. Naw ... I doubt it.

Well, you'll probably be pleased to find out that I'm trying desperately to change my ways. Maybe (just

171

maybe) I'm starting to take some of my 'lectric fence lessons to heart. Because I'm kind of a slow reader, Will's first option will take way too much time to see any results, but the one about observation ... now, I think even a one-eyed guy should be able to sort of figure that one out after while.

So ... in my quest to shape this camp up a little, I decided to do a little observation of some of the better run outfits around here and then try to figure out how they're doin' things. Tumbleweed Teddy and the TP Bar crew are right up there at the top of the list, so I've been sneakin' around and observin' some of the finer points of their operation.

We don't have time here to give you the whole scoop on how Ol' Tumbleweed got his name, but it happened a few years ago when the tumbleweeds got to rollin' off his outfit so bad that they plugged up the road that runs by the old TP Bar. The county road boys had to take a big V snowplow or a dozer or somethin' to clear the mess out.

It was quite a sight. The dang things were at least ten feet deep in places. The only reason that the traffic wasn't backed up for miles is that there wasn't any. That doggone road was completely impassible for quite a while, and he's been Tumbleweed Teddy ever' since.

I happened to bump into that outfit trailin' their two year old heifers down the road the other day, and that's when my newly trained techniques of observation kicked in. I got to noticin' Tumbleweed's crew. He's always got the best help in the country when he works cattle or goes to move 'em. I've never seen the like of it anyplace.

There are always at least a couple of brand in-spectors ridin' for him every time. There are a few things that the Department of Livestock comes up with that I probably don't agree with, but in all my vast years of experience, I've never seen one of those State Brand Inspectors that wasn't a heck of a hand, and here they are ridin' for the TP Bar ... for free. I set out to find out how he pulls that off.

A lot of fellas just don't like to ask for help, and us 'lectric fence types are usually the worst of the bunch. But ... if someone calls you up and offers to help, now that's a different story. I think Ol' Tumbl-weed has a few 'lectric fence tendencies too, so the only thing I can figure is these guys are just callin' him up and volunteering their services.

Why would they do that, you ask? That's a dang good question. The only thing I can figure is that they're tryin' to catch him red handed with a critter that might not be entirely his.

He's a sly old fox, that Tumbleweed. He acts like he doesn't even know what's goin' on when the brand inspectors are constantly ridin' up to the point (one on each side) and then slowly working their way back to the rear of the herd letting the cattle trail past them. It would be obvious to most any durn fool that they're checkin' the brands, but he doesn't even seem to notice. THAT'S the way to get a good crew to trail your cows.

What they don't know is Ol' Tumbleweed was up at midnight the night before with a flashlight, stash-in' all the critters in the brush that he didn't want them to see. The obvious secret here is to spread just enough rumors around down at the coffee shop to make the brand boys suspicious. The hard part is making sure they don't figure out where your brush patch stash is.

I just happened to have a couple of round bales on the pickup when I ran into those guys on the trail the other day, and one of the inspectors rode up to me and says with a half a grin and a nod towards the bales, "Sure looks like stolen hay to me."

Boy, now those brand boys are some sharp cookies. As a matter of fact, I HAD just "borrowed" one itty-bitty load from my brother (Fearless Frank) ... but, how in the dickens did he know that? Maybe I just look guilty... like Tumbleweed does. It's more than likely just the permanently contorted look a fella gets on his face after a couple o' jillion confrontations with a 'lectric fence.

I'll probably never figure this deal all out. All I know for sure is that I must not have the art of observation quite mastered yet. If I did, I would've tapped one of those big haystacks over at the TP Bar.

A fella 'd never get caught in one of their hay corrals when the whole crew is ten miles away trailin' cows ... with half the law in the county helpin' 'em.

"If ya ask me Dick, I think Ol' Tumbleweed is flirtin' with the undertaker. The further I can stay away from them Brand Boys the better I like it."

Chapter
Thirty Five

Watch Out For Lightnin'

"Well, I'll be doggoned," Dick hiccupped one morning as he opened up an official looking envelope. "Look-ee here what I got in the mail. Says I got picked fer jury duty. Wonder what that amounts to?"

"Prob'ly beats fixin' fence," his pal Billy sympathized, as he winged an empty can into the thirty gallon drum on the porch of their old shack. "Sounds sort of int'restin' to me. I never been on a jury, but my Uncle Lem was one time."

"Yea?"

"Uh-huh ... it was quite a deal, best I remember. Him an' Aunt Myrtle dang near split up over that one." Billy popped the top on another of Milwaukee's finest.

"Yer kiddin'."

"Nope. In fact it liked t' split the whole community right down the middle." Billy takes a long pull off his fresh can and began his story in earnest.

175

"See, they lived way down South there someplace ... Kentucky 'r Tennessee, I think. Their place was in Calhoun County ... over sort of close to the Jefferson County line. Now, Calhoun County was one of them dry counties an' you could buy booze legal in Jefferson County."

"Never heard of such a thing," Dick snorted.

"Yep ... she's still that way down there, far as I know," Billy assured him.

"Well, Aunt Myrtle was purty religious an' she was brought up in a little white church house right down the road from their place. I think her Pa was even a deacon 'er somethin'.

I reckon that's where her an' Uncle Lem was married ... right there in that little white church house ... an' she went there real reg'ler. Uncle Lem, on the other hand, didn't ezacly toe the line all the time. Oh, he'd go with her ever' now an' again, but he didn't take all that stuff near as serious as Aunt Myrtle did.

What she didn't know was that Grandpa used to have a still up in a coulee ... they call 'em hollers down there ... when Uncle Lem was a kid, an' when Grandpa got too old to run it, Lem had took it over. He ran off ten 'er fifteen gallons a week up there, an' it didn't matter much to him if Calhoun County was dry 'er not, 'cause sellin' moonshine is again' the law EVERPLACE. ...didn't seem to slow him down much though, an' a dry county has even more customers than a wet one. If Aunt Myrtle ever knew 'bout that still and Lem's moonshine business she never let on.

Well, the problem all got started when Red Weatherby decided to build a tavern right across the Jefferson County line where one was legal, an' it

176

couldn't have been over a half a mile down the road from that little white church house. Those church folks had a fit, figgerin' that the whole community was goin' down the drain, but there just wasn't any way they could stop it. Uncle Lem didn't think too much of the idea either, as it was bound to cut into his business some.

Well, all those church folks had this big prayer meetin', and I guess they was prayin' an' carryin' on down there fer a day er two straight. Ol' Red had the tavern buildin' all built an' was figgerin' on havin' a big Grand Openin' the very next weekend. I'll be doggoned if a big storm didn't blow up and lightnin' struck that brand new buildin' an' burned the durn thing right to the ground."

"Naw!" Dick scoffed skeptically.

"Yep, did so," Billy confidently replied.

"Well ol' Red was fit to be tied. His bran' new tavern was burned down, an' he figgered them prayin' church folks was directly responsible, so he took 'em to court and sued 'em fer the damages, an' Uncle Lem wound up on the jury."

"What happened?" Dick questioned.

"Doggone it, I don't really remember how it all turned out for sure, but somehow durin' the investigation, Aunt Myrtle found out about Lem's little distillery an' the shine he'd been peddlin' all those years, an' she dang near tied a can on his tail."

"What about the trial ... THAT'S what I want to know," Dick questioned, prying for more information.

"Well, Red told the judge that the church folks was prayin' again' him and caused the storm to come up an' the lightnin' to strike, and so it was their fault. On the other hand, the church folks claimed they didn't have nuthin' to do with it. They admitted they was havin' a prayer meetin', and that they MIGHT have said a prayer or two about the new den of iniquity just down the road, but they didn't have nuthin' to do with no lightnin'. They said that was just a coincidence."

"How'd it turn out?"

"Don't 'member. All I recollect is Uncle Lem's comment about the judge. He declared that he'd never run into a case like this in his whole life, and makin' a rulin' was gonna be tough. It looked for all the world to him that they had to decide between a tavern owner that believed in the power of prayer, even though he claimed he hardly ever prayed, and a whole church full of folks that prayed all the time but didn't believe it really worked."

"Personally, I pray all the time. It's just over the hill to Ronald McDonald's, you know."

Chapter Thirty Six

Fearless Frank's Close Call

*T*hey say that truth is stranger than fiction ... well, I think "they" are on to something. We've all heard a thousand tired old jokes about a cowboy with his pants down having an encounter with a rattlesnake. Thank Goodness it's never ever happened to me, but it did to my brother "Fearless Frank" not long ago. Although it could have turned out a whole lot worse than it did, here's how this deal came down.

Frank and a couple of his boys had a bunch of cows that needed a change of pasture, so their day started about daylight. It had been hot as blazes, and because those critters just don't trail worth beans after the sun gets too high in the sky, a good early start in the morning is the only way to get 'er done.

Well, this particular day the boys got rolling just like they should have and had the cows and calves to the fresh new field of grass by mid-morning. It went without a hitch, and as they eased them through the gate, Ol' Fearless even came up with the right number. What a deal.

"That wasn't so tough," he thought to himself. "I'm glad that job is over with."

It was then that he remembered another "job" that he'd forgotten in his haste to get the cows on the road that morning. Yep, Mother Nature blatantly issued her infamous call.

We can all remember times when Mother Nature's summons was a whole lot less than convenient to answer, but this really wasn't one of them. The cattle were all moved, and had their heads down grazing away on the fresh grass, and he was way out on the prairie so there weren't any privacy issues to deal with.

I'll try to deal with this very serious subject matter as delicately as possible ... just stick with me. Remember ... "Truth IS stranger than fiction," and this is just what happened.

Fearless Frank shut the pasture gate and commenced to answer the call he'd received right there by the corner post. Unfortunately, he didn't know there was a big fat rattlesnake just a few feet away whose morning nap had been all messed up by a hundred head of cows stompin' right through his front yard. Now, Mr. Snake had taken all of that abuse without saying a word, but when the disgusting view of the south end of an exposed cowboy was piled on top of his previous morning's experience, it was just more than he could take.

"Bzzzzzzzzzzssssssszzzzzzsssss."

That's a sound that will strike a chord of fear in the bravest of hearts, never mind a chicken liver like "Fearless Frank." I maybe forgot to mention

180

that Frank tends to be a little on the excitable side. Well, this time he really had something to be excited about.

His entire life flashed before his eyes in a split second. He even caught a glimpse of his own obituary and how the newspaper had graciously omitted the location of the fatal snake bite.

"How far do you think you can jump from this position with your jeans around your ankles?" Fearless asked me as he squatted down in our kitchen relating the story.

That's a hard question to answer, but given the proper amount of motivation, a fella can probably make a pretty good sized hop. Nobody knows if the snake ever took a strike at him or not, (I doubt if even a snake would lower himself to THAT level), and apparently Frank didn't bother looking over his shoulder to see.

As I mentioned earlier, this all turned out a whole lot better than it could have. Fearless Frank didn't get snake bit. But ... in addition to the scare of his life, there were a few additional negative consequences.

Maybe you recall the story about the time that he was attacked by the deranged Curlew? That was really scary. The bird flew in the pickup window and tried to peck him to death. He almost wrecked the pickup and he DID wet his pants.

Let me suffice to say that this was a worse mess than that one ... a LOT worse.

... and you'll have to figure out for yourself where all of those cactus spines wound up.

"I'll tell ya somethin', Dick. I got no idea how in the dickens he'd get a nickname like "Fearless Frank". Anytime a fella lets a little thing like a rattlesnake mess up somethin' that important, it looks to me like "Chicken Liver Frank" would fit a whole lot better."

Chapter
Thirty Seven

Stealin' From a Thief

I suppose most everyone has had something stolen from them some time or other. If you haven't ... just hang on to your hat, your turn's probably coming. It can certainly be frustrating, that's for sure, but I want to tell you about a time that a guy had something stolen from him, and it actually turned out for the best. As a matter of fact, it probably kept him out of the crow bar hotel. Here's the story:

Back in the sixties, Wellington D. Rankin had a very extensive ranching empire across Montana. He was a fancy pants lawyer and a politician and some sort of kin folk to Jeanette Rankin, the first woman to ever be elected to the US House of Representatives. From strictly an investment perspective, he probably came out just fine, but his ranch management style was a little lacking. He bought out the huge Miller Brothers Ranch here in the northern part of the state in the late fifties, and life as we knew it here changed forever.

Because he ran things with low inputs (very little decent help), the shear magnitude of the ranch was impossible for the few capable guys there to handle. It got to be a real joke. If you happened to border him, as did almost everyone in this neck of the woods, the fence was just yours to fix. That wasn't always a problem, as sometimes the pastures didn't even get used. Unfortunately, there were many other times when there were too many cattle on too few acres for too long. What a wreck.

When moving the large cow herds from one pasture to another, the Rankin operation would leave orphaned calves every place. Some of his jaded neighbors began to help themselves to the orphans to "even up" on the fence he didn't fix. After all, many of the baby calves would have died if they hadn't taken them home. A few of the more entrepreneurial buckaroos (many without a score to settle) began to help themselves too, not even waiting for the calves to be orphaned. Anything that wasn't branded was considered fair game. After all, they were just stealin' from a lawyer, and one that had it comin' to boot. Things got totally out of control.

When the news got back to Mr. Rankin that folks were stealin' his cattle, he wasn't all that impressed. Apparently, he didn't think it was nearly as funny as everyone else did. He got his tail in a knot and promptly contacted the Department of Livestock to call out the stock inspectors. He really raised a ruckus, and his high political connections probably increased the urgency a little.

Although a lot of the locals knew who some of the prime suspects were, it took the brand boys a while to get to the bottom of things. One enterprising young cowboy, that I'll call Jack, often times hauled his stolen calves around in a short little trailer house, and that little trick of his had been workin' for quite some time. After all, the brand inspector might pull over someone in a pickup with a stock rack wrapped in canvas, but who in the world would suspect a guy that looked like he was just goin' campin'?

One day Jack was breezing down the highway with a load of contraband like he'd done so many times before, and I'll be doggoned if he didn't blow out a tire. No spare. Apparently things don't always go according to the plan for cattle rustlers either. He didn't have much choice but to drop the trailer by the side of the road while he went back to town for a new tire.

Seeing the trailer on the shoulder of the road, one of our trusty highway patrolmen stopped to check things out. He found a little more than he expected. Here was a trailer house all jacked up with one of the wheels off, but it was jiggling around on the jack, and there were little moo-ing sounds coming from inside. A peek in a window revealed the contents, and his investigative mind precipitated a call to the stock inspectors to see if perhaps the calves therein were stolen.

The brand boys were elated. It was the big break they'd been waiting for. Jack had been on their suspect list for quite sometime, but now they finally had the evidence they needed to nail him. All they had to do was stake out the trailer, and when Jack came back with the new tire, they had him.

It was getting late in the afternoon, and as the sun was going down, they found a spot right across the road from the trailer where they could hide themselves in some brush behind a little hill. Catchin' the culprit with the goods was just a matter of time.

Darkness fell and still no one showed up to put the wheel back on. Midnight came and went, and finally as the dawn was breaking, the two bleary eyed stock inspectors stumbled sleepily from their hiding place across the highway to check out the trailer.

It was empty.

From their vantage point in the brush behind the hill, they couldn't see the trailer house door, which happened to be on the other side. Sometime during the night, some OTHER industrious individuals of questionable character had recognized the trailer beside the highway, and had re-stolen the calves from the first thief ... right under the noses of the stock inspectors. This sort of sounds like a bad old Laurel & Hardy movie, doesn't it?

When Jack showed back up to put his tire on, his new calves were gone, but coincidently so was all of the thievin' evidence. As a result, he managed to keep his foot out of the trap the brand boys had so carefully set for him. He was one lucky duck.

They say that it ain't even a sin to steal from a thief. Although that sounds sort of logical, I'm not totally convinced that's the case. One thing I know for sure ... it would probably be a good idea for those boys to have a good story cooked up when they get to the Pearly Gates ... just in case they have a hard question or two to answer.

Chapter Thirty Eight

Paybacks Can Be A Bummer

$\mathcal{S}$onny and Porky were the best of buddies, and had been all of their lives. They were born down in the middle of Montana someplace in the late '20s. Growing up in the midst of the Great Depression was something they just thought was normal, so they got used to making their own fun.

Sometimes I think we have way too much "stuff" nowadays, and as a result, miss out on the creativity required to have a good time with absolutely no money. As the lyrics to an old song go; "We all heard that Wall Street fell, but we were broke and couldn't tell." One thing's for sure, the probable lack of "foldin' money" didn't seem to hamper those two boys any ... at least if half the stories I've heard are true.

Porky was a town kid, and was always bummin' around out at Sonny's. There was always something to do out on the ranch, and it was an exciting place to grow up. Getting any work out of those two when they were young must have been quite a challenge. My Grandad had a saying he used to use when being blessed with a lot of "help" like that.

This is how he measured up his crew: He said, "A boy is a boy, two boys is half a boy, and three boys is no boy at all." Although he had me and a couple of my pals in mind the first time I heard that, I've seen that old sayin' proven numerous times by some of the "help" we've had around here through the years.

Well, even though they were known far and wide for having a good time, they were also responsible enough that they were given the job of moving a bunch of cows to the high country one spring. After all, they WERE ten or eleven years old. Responsibility comes early to country kids.

What an adventure. The boys packed some lunch on their saddles, grabbed their rifles, and headed the cows out the gate. It was a long steep climb up to the summer range. There's no better method to grow boys up than to let them know that they're being trusted to do a man's job.

Although there were still snow banks in the deep coulees, it was a nice warm spring day. The sun was warm on their peach fuzz cheeks, and by mid afternoon when they'd finally reached the top of a long flat ridge, the cattle were needing a rest, and the lunch the boys had packed seemed to be calling their names.

They unsaddled their horses to air out their backs and hobbled them to graze on the flush of new spring grass. With the combination of warm sunshine, tired bones, and a full stomach, a nice little nap was the obvious next item on the agenda.

Porky was nudged out of his little snooze by some strange noises. He lazily cracked one eyelid enough to see where they was coming from. It was just Sonny.

"Wonder why he's makin' those funny little sounds?" he thought to himself.

When he finally got both eyes open from his lazy afternoon doze to take a serious look at his pardner, he figured it out right away. There, big as life, right in the middle of Sonny's chest was a rattlesnake! I guess snakes can probably sense the extra heat, and had crawled out of his nearby snake hole for a little sunshine and was drawn to the warmth of Sonny's body.

Oh, boy. Sonny was scared spit-less and the terrified little sounds he was making were to wake up his friend without (hopefully) upsetting his uninvited bed partner. Porky's reaction was quick and immediate. Depression raised kids learned to think on their feet at a young age.

"He went instantly to get his gun," you're guessing.

Wrong. He went to grab his camera out of the saddle bags.

"Nobody would have believed that story ... we HAD to have a picture or two."

As soon as he'd taken a few shots from various angles to make certain that they'd have a good one

to save for posterity, Porky at long last did get one
of the rifles. There would probably be nothing much
worse than either of these alternatives:

1. He'd not make a killing shot and the snake
would bite his buddy several miles from help, or ...

2. He'd miss AND shoot his buddy in the chest,
AND he'd get snake bit, AND they'd still be several
miles from help.

Soooo ... with these two very poor scenarios firmly
planted in his mind, Porky was ever so careful to
keep Sonny's ribs out of the line of fire and to get
the snakes attention focused on the gun barrel. He
finally managed. Snakes will do that, you know ...
they'll look right down a gun barrel if you take your
time.

190

"KERPOW!"

It was a perfect shot. The only real casualties, (from everyone's perspective except Mr. Snake's) were the big mess on Sonny's face caused by flying reptile parts, and a nearly lost friendship. Yes, Porky had very likely saved his life ... BUT, "He dang shore didn't have to take a picture first!"

It was years later when Sonny finally got even. He was an accomplished roper, and although Porky had roped a few things on foot, his old friend was going to initiate him into calf roping, rodeo style. After a few last minute instructions, Porky mounted up to ride into the box.

"Just a minute," his cowboy friend called. "I better fix that." Sonny reached behind Porky's leg to make a last minute adjustment to the saddle.

Porky thought it was tightening the cinch. Nope ... he loosened it. (What are friends for?) The victim caught his calf, Sonny's rope horse hit the brakes, and the whole outfit (calf, rope, saddle, and Porky) went out over the horse's head into a big pile in the middle of the arena.

What fun ... ain't paybacks a bummer?

Women

Now, I know some stuff about women
Though you might think I'm a hick
There was a time, when I's in my prime
I'd run 'em off with a stick

Though it's true that I'm handsome
An' my humility's a matter of pride
You may wonder why, such a wonderful guy
Never wound up with a bride

Well, I've had plenty o' chances
When 'round the dance hall I'm lurkin'
But when the love bug bit, I played hard t' get
An' I want ya t' know that it's workin'

192

Chapter
Thirty Nine

Fresh Hot Dogs

*F*red and Martha Olson were just salt of the earth kind of folks. They spent their lives in the cattle business on the north slope of the Bear Paw Mountains of northern Montana. Fred was only sixteen when he boarded a ship in Sweden that was bound for America. He landed here in the early 1900's with a strong back, no money, and unable to speak English ... but he knew how to work. Apparently that was enough, as he taught himself to read and write English and did very well in business.

Martha was a real beauty, and the oldest of several children. Her father was a Jewish merchant in several of the early Montana boom towns, and her mom was of English descent. In fact, the rumor is that her mother's family nearly disowned her for marrying someone that "wasn't one of us."

Fred and Martha had a wonderful life and a house full of kids, but it wasn't without its struggles. Martha's mother had died when she was quite young and by default she became the surrogate mom to her younger brothers and sisters, having them to raise as well as her own growing brood. Her dad was quite a gambler with a reputation that wasn't always the most savory. He was rich one day and broke the next ... several different times. He wound up blind and penniless in his old age with no place to go, so Fred and Martha took him in as well. That little house in the Bear Paws must have been literally running over.

Making a living with all of those mouths to feed was quite a challenge. There were still large expanses of open range in the early 1900's, and Fred made a few dollars taking in cattle to pasture. He homesteaded a strategic spot on Clear Creek where the creek bottom is pinched between the steep slopes of the mountains on each side. Here with the bottom less than a hundred yards across, he was able to fence out his homestead and protect all the open range up the creek from the large numbers of Sprinkle Ranch Company cattle that were headquartered a few miles downstream.

It was too much work for the cattle to climb the steep hills and go around the end of the fence to get to the thousands of acres of free grass up in the higher country, so very few ever did. If any happened to stray around the end, it was pretty easy to kick them back down through the fence into the creek bottom for home. Consequently, there were miles and miles of green grass and good water that needed grazing, and Fred took in a lot of cattle. It was a good stroke of business on his part. Fred Olson was a pretty sharp cookie.

With it being 30 miles or so, going to town was a pretty rare and special occasion. The cars weren't as reliable and the tires not nearly as good in the early years, and with every trip into the city the sharp shale rocks could be counted on to deliver a flat tire or two.

In fact, it was a real possibility that they might not even make it home on the same day that they left. A house full of kids, a barn full of milk cows, and a coop full of chickens meant someone had to be home for chores EVERY evenin', so consequently when a trip was necessary, Fred often just went alone. Besides, everyone wouldn't fit into the old rattle trap car anyway.

He was about halfway through the trek into town one fine day about 1930 or so when he hears a little rustle in the back seat. He turned around to find Harry, the youngest of his boys hiding in the back. Going to

Mischievous Harry Olson

town was a big deal for a country boy of five or six years old, and Harry already knew what the answer would be if he asked to go along, so he tried the old stowaway trick.

It worked. Fred was too far from home to turn around, so after getting a good scolding Harry climbed over into the front seat ... grinning like a skunk eatin' onions. I've often wondered what poor Martha must have thought. There were no phones to call home and tell her where her missing kid was. Heck, it was still over twenty years before they'd even have electricity. She must have been beside herself with worry.

Harry has always liked hotdogs. They were quite a treat in the old days when all the meat was home butchered and nobody took the time to make them. They were a "town treat," and I'm sure the little stinker must have been buggin' his Dad all the way to town to get him one.

The Krezelak family ran a slaughter house and butcher shop in Havre. Harry KNEW they'd have a hotdog if he could just talk his Dad into stopping by there before they headed back for the hills. Sure enough, Harry was quite a salesman as a young fella, and kind-hearted ol' Dad was over being mad, so he agreed.

The butcher shop was quite a sight for those young eyes. After hearing the story about needing a hotdog, Mr. Krezelak gave Harry the bad news.

"Sorry, Sonny. We're all out of hotdogs …. but I guess I could take the time to make a few more for you."

With that, the kind old butcher scooped up one of the fat little puppies lying in a nearby nest with his mother and put him in a hole in his "hotdog machine" he'd created just for gullible little country kids. The puppy slid down a chute and safely into a padded box inside the fabricated wooden contraption, out of sight of the big eyed country boy, while the butcher turned a huge crank on the front of his "machine."

Out came a long string of hotdogs all hooked together on the ends like they were in those days, and suddenly young Harry was torn between his love for puppies and hotdogs. He had no idea that's where they came from.

"Holy cow! So that's why they call 'em hotdogs," Harry hesitantly thought to himself, as his five year old brain made a desperate attempt to process all this new information. Eventually his love for the "town treat" of hotdogs won out.

"Oh well," he reasoned philosophically to himself, "… at least they're fresh."

It was quite a trick. I've heard that some of those green country kids were twenty years old before they figured out it was a joke.

Chapter Forty

The Modern Aero-matic Doohickey

It finally rained over at Dick & Billy's hard luck outfit. The combination of all the green grass and grease wood were really makin' the boys feel prosperous. The branding was all done, and the cows actually had something to eat for a change.

"Doggone it Billy," Dick offered as they lounged on the porch with a few bottles of Milwaukee's finest, just watching the raindrops plunking down in the puddles. "We need to fix this outfit up a little. Soon as it quits rainin' maybe we oughta see about fixin' the roof on the barn."

"Yea, prob'ly so," Billy hiccupped as he squinted over at their dilapidated old barn. "There's even pigeons goin' in an' out of a couple of them holes."

Dick stuck a fresh wad of snooze under his lip, and continued with the plan he'd had rattlin' around in his head the last few days. "Las' time I wuz in town, ol' Art at the hardware store said he had one o' them new fangled aero-matic nail guns, an' he'd let us rent it fer almost nuthin'. You jus' hook 'er up to the air compressor and pull the trigger an' nails jus' fly out the end as fast as ya can pull the trigger. It'll be the real deal fer up on that steep roof."

"Aero-matic nail gun my foot. Dumbest thing I ever heard of," Billy belched. "We got a couple o' hammers already ... an' you don't even have to hook 'em up to no air compressor."

"Yea, I know," Dick defended his brainy idea, "but one o' them new outfits 'd free up yer hand that you gotta use to hold the nails, so there ain't as much danger o' fallin' off the roof. That sucker's purty steep an' I'll betcha it's slicker 'n the dickens up there."

"Well, I don't want nuthin' to do with no aero-matic nuthin'," Billy smirked. "That's ezac'ly what's the matter with America. Dang that progress anyway. Ever'body thinks they gotta have some aero-matic doohickey t' do the same job that a plain ol' hammer's been doin' fer a thousan' years."

The boys never did see eye to eye on that one, so later that day when it had dried up enough to tackle the gumbo trail to town, Dick wound up over at the hardware store and picked up that fancy aero-matic nail gun that Art had told him about.

"You don't have t' have nuthin' to do with it," he indignantly offered as Billy shot him one of those.... "yer as bad as all the rest of them modern knuckle-heads," looks.

After a stop over at the grocery store, and down at the feed store for a few blocks of salt, the boys swung by the clothing store so Billy could buy himself a brand new overall jacket. (I told you they were feeling prosperous.)

The next morning they dug up a few old bent pieces of tin that had blown off one of the other buildings and tied into their project. They put a ladder in the bucket of their old John Deere loader tractor so they could reach high enough to get on the roof of the ancient old barn, and Dick threw a rope over the ridge and tied it off to a railroad tie corral post ... "just in case." He also wheeled the air compressor over close and strung out the extension cord.

Billy just rolled his eyes. He still wasn't impressed. He grabbed an old hammer and stuck a handful of nails in the pocket of his new jean jacket and up to the roof they went, each of them dragging a sheet of tin.

The first sheet or two went pretty slow. Gettin' the hang of a new job always seems to go that way, but Dick's new nail gun was working like a dream, even if it WAS just "unnecessary progress" in Billy's opinion.

The morning air was filled with the "Kerwump! Kerwump!" of Dick's nail gun, and the "Rappity-tap-tap ... OUCH!! ... %$#@!!" of Billy's hammer and the nastiest words you ever heard when he hit his thumb.

An hour or so into the job is when the disaster struck. On a particularly difficult piece of tin, Billy lost his balance and started sliding on the seat of his pants down the steep incline. With a handful of nails in one hand, a hammer in the other, and nothing but blue sky to grab on to, apparent catastrophe was just a few seconds and twenty some feet away.

Dick just happened to see his partner sliding helplessly to his doom, and by coincidence, had the "just in case" rope in one hand and the nail gun in the other. Billy was clawing at every nail and screw, trying to slow his descent, but was losing the battle. His feet were just sliding over the eaves when Dick managed to catch the collar of that new overall jacket with one hand while he desperately clung to the rope and the nail gun with the other.

Dangling out there in space, Billy's position was worse than precarious. Dick didn't have the strength to pull his partner back up the steep incline, so he did the next best thing. Quick as you please, he nailed the collar of that new jacket to the barn roof.

"Kerwhump! Kerwump! Kerwhump! Kerwhump!"

The heat of the moment had soon passed, and the sight of Billy hanging out there in the beautiful blue sky, held by nothing but the four nails in the collar of his overall jacket, was just about more than Dick could take. He got to laughin' so hard that he almost fell off the roof himself.

"NOW ... ," Dick hooted at his helpless partner, "do you want to take back all that stuff you said about them modern aero-matic doohickeys, 'er do you want me to jus' go ahead an' pull them nails out?"

Chapter
Forty One

Electric Antlers

*T*here's been a story circulating around these parts the last forty or fifty years or so about a wrestling match that a couple of Rural Electric linemen had with a mule deer buck. The problem with stories like that is they tend to get a little better with every telling.

When you add the fact that the two heroes of the story were regular visitors down at the Vet's Club after work, and if the rumors I heard were true, possibly ingested a couple of fermented barley beverages while there, it's easy to see how the story could possibly change over the course of time. Some of those liquids down at the Vet's Club can have varied and unpredictable results. A couple of beers can somehow make the biggest liar in town tell you the gospel truth, and then on the other hand, a normally honest man might just lie through his teeth.

This is my attempt to clear the air and the reputations of the men involved and to get down to the brass tacks of what actually happened. I took the majority of the facts from a newspaper clipping that reported the news at the time. Everyone knows newspaper men always tell the truth ... except I think maybe this one got his facts down at ... well, you know. There were a few spots where I couldn't make out the words on the old clipping, but I'm fairly certain what it must have said, so I'll just repeat what I'm sure was there.

The exact year is a little hard to pin down, (I couldn't make out the date) but it really doesn't matter all that much. It was around 1960 or so, give or take five or six years, and John Broesder and Ken Darlington were headed down the road south of Big Sandy, Montana to run a new power line to a pump out in the middle of Bob Brewer's hay field. As usual they were joshin' and teasing each other on the way there.

John Broesder
Fearless Buck Deer Wrestler

"I think we're only going to need to set a pole or two. This wouldn't be much of a job if a fella just had a little decent help," John smirked at his helper.

The two guys had worked together a lot through the years, and Ken was not one to be outdone in the teasing department.

"Help my foot," he snapped. "I could prob'ly out do you with one hand tied behind my back."

They both had a good laugh and at long last got to Brewer's hay meadow, and began to scope out the job to see just what needed to be done. They'd had

202

it figured about right, and only had to set a couple of poles to reach the well that required new electric service. They unrolled the wire and began to pace off the distance to decide where the poles should be.

Meanwhile, hidden in the willows on the edge of the hay field was an enormous mule deer buck suspiciously eyeing the intruders. The Brewer's had hand raised him from the time he was just a fawn, but that had been four or five years ago, so he now sported a huge five point rack of antlers. His tender bottle raising had left him with no natural fear of people, and with the fear gone, all that remained was an air of overconfident contempt for the strange arrogant humanoids that were suddenly tracking up his private domain.

John and Ken were busy counting the steps between poles and getting their job done, so they didn't even notice the huge muley in the brush shaking his head threateningly. Ken was perhaps fifteen or twenty yards ahead when John suddenly heard a sound behind them. Here came the buck on the charge, with his head down and the seat of John's pants in his sights.

John Broesder was no little guy; six foot two in his stockin' feet, and about 230 pounds in wrestlin' shape. Athough he was to later lose an arm in an electical accident, he was certainly no slouch. The biggest problem here was his lack of experience wrestling a five point muley that coincidently happened to tip the scale at about the same weight. He turned just in time to save a good horn pokin' and grabbed a handful of antlers, pushing them into the dirt.

It must have been quite a sight. I wish I'd have been there. It was one of those Mexican standoff deals with neither of the wrestlers able to gain much of an advantage. John would gain a little ground and then the buck would plant all four of those sharp hooves of his and push John back the other way a while.

When Ken heard the commotion, he was too busy laughing to be much help. A fella can see the danged-est things when he doesn't have a camera. By now John was losing his patience with his dilly-dallying partner and was desperately hollerin' for help. To be fair, he wasn't really losing the battle, but was scared to turn loose of the death grip he had on those antlers.

Ken finally got the tears of laughter wiped away long enough to give his partner a hand. He picked up a chunk of an old dead diamond willow at the edge of the field and waving it over his head and yellin' like a Comanche on the war path, he charged the big buck.

It worked. I doubt if that poor old mule deer had ever seen a deranged electric lineman before, so he cut and ran for the brush. He didn't run far, though.

"Those crazy guys may have won the first round," he thought to himself, "but they look an awful lot like the fella that fed me that bottle when I was a baby, so I ain't THAT scared of 'em."

John was pretty much exhausted. It had been quite a workout.

All the while the boys were finishing their job, Mr. Deer just stood there in the willows shaking his head threateningly, and looking like he'd charge again at any minute. Ken never did put down that war club.

As their job was nearing completion, John looked down from his safe perch on top of the utility pole at Ken standing near the base, with that diamond willow club still clutched in his hand, looking warily over his shoulder at the threatening five point buck.

"Outwork me with one hand tied behind your back, huh?" John jeered down from his place of safety. "Just as well tie it behind your back ... you ain't usin' it anyhow, and I'm up here doin' ALL the work."

Chapter
Forty Two

Watchin' Where You're Goin'

*T*hose unionized "paid-by-the-hour" types have got a lot of advantages over us daylight 'til dark, "go-'til-you-drop" country boys. After all, they even get paid, and some of them don't have to do all that much for their paycheck either. They also have the added benefit of not always having to be in a big hurry. They just don't HAVE to be. It's not their money they're wasting by going a little slower. Boy, that sure isn't the way she goes around here.

I remember a little incident a few years ago where I found myself afoot and a couple of miles from home. The tractor had broken down or something, and as usual, the work around here was at least two weeks behind. As I was hiking down the county road towards the home place, one of the neighbors drove up behind me.

I hadn't paid any attention, but I must have had my head down, pacin' like a Tennessee Walker headed downhill ... on his way back to the barn. The neighbor stopped and gave me a lift home.

"I could tell from a quarter of a mile away that you weren't somebody's hired man."

"Yea??" I answered, not knowing what he was drivin' at.

"Yea," came the reply. "You were walkin' way too fast."

Being in a constant hurry just gets to be a habit with folks that have a lot of work to do, and not enough time to get it all done. Tommy (not his real name) is one of those guys ... always scratchin' dirt and in a big rush. His wife Angie is a little gal and always tearing around in a trot too. (That's not her real name either.) They're ranchers, and just don't have the time to let any grass grow under their feet.

There are several times I can think of that being in too big a hurry has been a huge mistake on our outfit, but I want to tell you about a couple of times it didn't turn out too good for Tommy & Angie either.

It was the early 70's sometime, and they had their two little boys loaded up in their old four wheel drive and were headed down the trail to put out some salt for the cows or something ... in a big hurry, of course. They got to a gate, and Tommy bailed out to open it. Angie would have gladly opened it, but she couldn't. Tommy had stretched the wire too tight when he built it.

Mistake number one. NEVER, I repeat NEVER, should a man build a gate that his wife can't open. That just doesn't make any sense ... but I digress. Back to the story:

They were on pretty flat ground, so Tommy just left the door open and the pickup running as he opened the gate, and then drove through and did the same on the other side as he was closing it behind them.

As her "always in a big rush" hubby was closing the gate, Angie thought this would be a perfect time to answer the call of nature she'd recently received by all the bouncing they'd done over the prairie. She slipped out her door and around in the front of the pickup for a little privacy.

In his haste, Tommy didn't even miss her when he got back in and closed the door. In Angie's nature call answering position in front of the tall four wheel drive, she was totally out of view. (Privacy at a time like that is a good thing, but just maybe a little better communication might not have hurt anything either.)

Tommy jammed the outfit in gear and took off. The boys were saying something, but his mind was cuttin' hay and fixin' fence, and he didn't pay any attention to them. Besides, those kids were always jabberin' about something.

Angie was about the business at hand when the pickup started forward, and had absolutely no warning or time to take defensive action.

"Mama, Mama, Mama!" one of the boys yelled.

It was only then that Tommy figured out what they'd been trying to tell him all along. It was too late. He ran right smack over her. Angie rolled up under that old pickup like a basket ball ... with her bloomers down around her ankles. It's a dang wonder he didn't kill her or break her back or something, but by the Grace of God, other than being a little skinned up she was fine. Her small

207

size may have been the only thing that saved her. That near tragedy takes that old saying, "Gettin' the water scared out of you," to a whole new level.

A few years later it was Angie's turn to return the favor. She was the one driving the pickup this time, and was scheduled to meet up with Tommy at a certain spot in the pasture. He was out doing something with the cows on the four-wheeler. They were in pretty rough country and as stubby little Angie topped a hill, and couldn't see anything but blue sky over the hood of the pickup, she had no way of knowing that her lovin' hubby was just over the crest.

The front bumper hit the back tires of the four-wheeler, and Tommy apparently must have accidentally hit the button on the ejection seat. The impact definitely helped the launch too, and he did a perfect swan dive thirty feet out into the sagebrush, landing in a big pile of tangled up cowboy.

To be perfectly honest, it's a wonder that either one of them are still alive. Angie's "Mother Nature" accident could certainly have been a whole lot worse, that's for sure.

But now that I think about it, just maybe Tommy had his deal comin'. If he'd been chasin' cows on a saddle horse like the Good Lord intended, instead of riding that dang four-wheeler, they could have avoided the entire problem. First, a horse doesn't have a noisy gas motor, so he would have heard the pickup coming, and second, with the increase in elevation he'd have gotten from bein' horseback, they would have been able to see each other easy as you please.

But then ... from Tommy's perspective ... maybe it's a little faster. Serves him right.

Chapter
Forty Three

Those Wonderful Little Pigs

*F*ollowing your dreams is ALWAYS worth it. If in the process, the goin' gets a little tough once in a while, it just seems to make the good times all that much sweeter. I suppose it would be nice to be able to start out on the top of the pile, and not have to work hard for what we get, but somehow I have a feeling it would be a hollow victory.

Let me give you a farm family story that really isn't all that atypical. We all can use a dose of encouragement now and then, and hearing how other folks have stuck with it when the times were sorta tough helps to spur us on when our trail gets a little on the rough side; especially if the story has a happy ending like this one does.

Tom and Judy got married and started their life together out on the farm with little but youth and a dream. They managed to rent some land with an old set of buildings on it, so with all of that youthful exuberance, they moved in. Even though this wasn't all that long ago, it just so happens there wasn't any electricity on this old abandoned place.

Although both of them had been raised with all the conveniences that the REA could provide, that didn't happen to be where they found the opportunity for their "start." Two fresh married kids with less of a vision wouldn't have even tied into it.

Judy had to learn how to operate the old ancient wood cook stove, and the hand pump on the end of the kitchen counter that only delivered cold water was also something completely new.

"Maybe we can fix this place up a little this fall, huh?" she asked her hubby from her knees on the floor next to the scrub brush and the mop pail. No matter how hard she tried, she just couldn't make the old pine boards on the kitchen floor look very good.

"I doubt it," Tom replied with a grin. "It WOULD be nice, but this first year or two are going to be pretty tight." He really hated to let her down like that, but facts were facts. Judy's dream of having their own place and making their own way was just as strong as his, so if she was discouraged she never let him know.

One night in mid summer, Judy had heated a big pot of water on the cook stove and crawled into the little square tin wash tub that doubled as a place to wash their clothes AND a bathtub. She'd just gotten on her clean clothes and was fussing around about what to have for supper, when Tom came banging in the screen door.

"Got time to give me a hand?" he questioned. "That old sow just went in the barn and I shut the door on her and the pigs. It'd be a good time to take 'em away from her. They're sure needin' weaning."

Judy dutifully went out to help. If she had second thoughts because of her new clean clothes and perfumed hair, she never said anything. After all, this was HER dream, too.

Things didn't go well. They say that you never want to get between a sow grizzly and her cubs. Fortunately, I've never found myself in that position, but I HAVE been between a six or seven hundred pound sow pig and her babies a time or two, and it ain't a pretty sight. I can't see how a grizzly bear could be all that much worse. Either one of them will eat you if they get half a chance.

The plan was to cause enough confusion to distract the sow so that they could steal the babies one at a time, and then Tom would hand the piglets over the fence to Judy who put them into a cutoff barrel where they could hold them until they could be transferred into the special new pen they'd built. There were several extenuating circumstances that made the plan a little less than ideal.

First of all, Mama Sow wasn't all that impressed. Oh, the first one caught pretty easily, but the little buzzards have a tendency to squeal when you pick them up, so after kidnapping number one, Mama was on to the plan. For Tom, just keeping from being eaten was a full time job.

Then there was the keeping the piggies in the cut off barrel issue. The first couple were pretty easy, because she could just hold them by a hind leg, but after she got her hands full, Judy got pretty busy. Because they had free range of the place with lots of room to roam around, the little porkers were pretty clean when they went into the barn, but after locking them in the part of the barn where they milked the cows (complete with a gutter full of soupy digested green grass), they weren't quite clean enough to take to the county fair any longer.

The piggies were making frantic squealy laps around the cow barn, only pausing long enough for an occasional swan dive into the gutter on the way by. Tom would lunge down from his perch on the top of the stanchions at every opportunity and snare another prize; each one being slicker and greener than the one before.

Although it was safe on Judy's side of the fence, her job wasn't any easier. The poor gal wound up on her tummy, spread eagled across the top of that barrel with slick, squealing manure covered little pigs trying to escape every chance they got.

But ... "all's well that ends well." They finally got the pigs weaned, and took their filthy clothes off outside on the porch. Judy slipped back into the dirty ones she'd taken off before her bath, and quietly began to heat another tub of water.

"You know somethin', hun?" Tom offered as he poured himself a cup of coffee from the pot that was always brewing on the back of the old range. "I was doin' some figurin', and I think come this fall, those eight pigs we just weaned ought to buy us some linoleum for this ol' kitchen."

Tom and Judy are still chasing their dream, and it's still worth it. You'll be happy to learn that they've had electricity for quite sometime now.

Chapter
Forty Four

Marie Gibson, Lady Bronc Rider

*M*arie Gibson's dynamic career as a bronc and trick rider began with Havre, Montana's 1917 Great Northern Stampede and ended with her death at a 1933 Idaho Falls rodeo. The five-foot, four-inch tall, 135 pound, blue-eyed wonder with a distinctive French accent was a transplant to Havre from western Canada. She went on to win top money in rodeos, big and small, throughout the U.S., western Canada, and England.

Marie's parents migrated from Belgium to Holland, Manitoba, Canada where she was born on August 18, 1894. After a short term return to Belgium, the Massoz family settled in Saskatchewan.

It was there Marie learned the ways of ranching and handling horses and cattle. Besides farming, Mr. Massoz ran a livery stable where Marie helped gentle horses as saddle mounts and helped train race horses.

Her parents later moved to the United States, but Marie remained in Canada and married. At 16 her first child Lucien was born. Three years later, she and her family followed her parents lead, and settled at Burnham, along the Milk River about 10 miles west of Havre, Montana.

Marie Gibson
World Champion Lady Bronc Rider

Unfortunately, the marriage failed and her husband Joe Dumont returned to Canada. Marie stayed on at the ranch and kept her family of now three children going by working in Havre while her parents watched the youngsters.

During the turmoil and hardships, she became acquainted with her neighbor, "Long" George Francis and his friends, Ray Ellis, Jack Maybee and Clayton Jolley. Marie would stop at his ranch and watch the boys break wild horses to use for saddle and team animals. Soon, with their encouragement, Marie was riding bucking broncos herself.

In 1917 she entered the Francis and Maybee produced Great Northern Montana Stampede, winning third money in the horse racing event. At this show she first met Englishman Tom Gibson, who was a top Canadian bronc rider from the Red Deer, Alberta area. They met again at Canadian rodeos and eventually married. Tom's bronc riding career was cut short when he was run down by a drunken driver in 1923, and his health deteriorated even further after contracting TB.

From that first rodeo in Havre, Gibson plunged into the North American rodeo circuit and began the long hard bruising climb to the title of World Champion Cowgirl Bronc Rider. After Havre, Marie participated in Canadian rodeos at Nelson, B.C., Medicine Hat, Calgary, Moose Jaw, Regina and all stops in between. Later, she would travel all over the United States, competing in every major show in the country.

A big boost to her career came at the Saskatoon rodeo in 1919. There she won the Best Woman Bronc Rider award, quite an honor for a comparative newcomer. That particular show was attended by English royalty, and after winning her award, Marie

215

was escorted to the Royal Pavilion where she had a personal audience with the Prince of Wales, who would eventually be crowned King Edward VIII. Although honored to meet the "handsome young man," Marie was appalled at her dirty and disheveled appearance, and had wished she'd had time to clean up a little first.

The next major highlight of her rodeo career occurred in 1923 at the first of Tex Austin's New York City rodeos. Only the best riders in North America were invited for the nine-day show. The following spring, Austin made arrangements to take his performers to London for the 30-day British Empire Exhibition at Wembley Stadium.

Marie performed her usual trick and bronc riding everyday in spite of sustaining several injuries which would have put a lesser person in the hospital. While touring England with the traveling "Wild West Show" she had the opportunity to meet the Prince of Wales again (as well as the Queen of England) while attending a party at Buckingham Palace. This time she undoubtedly had the time to be a little more "presentable," but obviously had made a better initial impression than she'd thought, as the Prince well remembered their meeting several years earlier.

Although still on the mend from the injuries sustained in England, upon her return Marie participated in the Cheyenne Frontier Days rodeo in Wyoming and won the Women's World Bronc Riding Championship. She also won two additional World Championship titles at Madison Square Garden in New York City.

By 1930, she had grown weary of the tough demanding rodeo life. Even though she was reportedly earning 5000 dollars a year on the circuit (a lot of

Marie Gibson, Trick Rider

money in the 1920's), many of her rodeo performer friends had been killed along the way to stardom. She planned to quit the rodeo circuit when her two sons, Lucien and Buster completed high school (daughter Lucy had died) and settle down on their ranch.

But those dreams never materialized, for her career ended on September 23, 1933 at Idaho Falls. She was only 39. She had just completed an event when the pickup man's horse and Gibson's collided. Her horse crashed to the ground, and the head injuries she sustained resulted in her death a few hours later.

The Pendleton Roundup, one of the nation's largest rodeos had ended the lady bronc riding event after another champion rider, Bonnie McCarroll, had hung up in a stirrup and was drug to death in 1929. The other major rodeos soon followed suit, and lady bronc riding was history. It was the end of an era.

Reincarnation

I don't believe in reincarnation
Though some folks claim that it's true
I was told, they'll be streets of gold
But they say we'll wake up somethin' new

The thought to me is disturbing
The scariest thing that I've heard
If I wake up a horse, I could fake it of course
But what if I'm a fish or a bird

And what about you my cowboy friend?
To you I offer this vow
I'll teach you to moo, and suckle calves too
If perchance you wake up a cow

Chapter Forty Five

Sober Incentive

Ol' Bob used to be the town drunk in one of Montana's larger cities a few years ago, and although in a big town there's quite a bit of competition, he still had the title pretty well sewed up. I think he had a cell with his very own name on it down at the hoosegow. Because he was a terrible nasty drunk and always in trouble, the boys in blue would get called out at least twice a month to "Take care of Bob ... again," and back to the slammer he'd go.

Sober he was a pretty nice fella, but booze had a way of bringing out the monster in him. It's funny how that stuff affects different folks in different ways. Some people get silly, and others might just go to sleep, but Ol' Bob always got on the fight.

Well, apparently that's all changed. He hasn't been in any trouble for at least ten years. That boy is as straight as an arrow, now. Here's the story:

George and Chip are a couple of old timers on the police force, and have seen it all. They've really been around the block, those two. Through the years they've sort of allowed their overactive imaginations and perverted sense of humor to have a completely free rein. They say it helps preserve their sanity in an obviously high pressure line of work, but because of their apparent lack of restraint, things have sometimes been known to get a little out of hand.

Donny was a new rookie, and as such, was assigned to the two old guys on his first few days on the job. They cooked up a brand new plan to break the kid into the realities of law enforcement. The three were in their squad car when a call came in from headquarters ... it was Bob again. They pulled up to the little skid row bar where Ol' Bob was certain he could whip the whole outfit, and shortly had him cuffed and in the back seat of the patrol car. Donny was the rookie, so had to ride in the back with stinky Bob.

They were just headed back down the street to book their oft returning guest into his usual suite at the crowbar hotel, when their radio went off again.

"Armed robbery in progress! Liquor store at the corner of Second and Minnesota! Suspect is wearing a white shirt and baseball cap!"

Because they were only a few blocks away, they turned on their siren and the bubble gum machine light on the top of their car and sped to the scene, giving Donny strict instructions to stay in the car to watch Bob. They had just screeched to a halt in front of the store when out ran the suspect in a white shirt.

"There he comes! That's him!" yelled George with his pistol drawn. "Halt! Police!"

Here, the story gets a little fuzzy. Whether the guy stopped or turned to run away, I'm not sure, but George and Chip both unloaded on him, each getting off three or four rounds.

220

"He's dead," Chip whispered to his partner as he looked down at the blood spattered white shirt.

"Man ... maybe we shouldn't have shot him! I don't see a gun! We're gonna be in big trouble!"

"Quick! Let's load him in the back of the car!"

The two veteran cops drug the dead victim to the back of the squad car and dumped his body in the trunk. The rookie's eyes were as big as a couple of silver dollars, and Ol' Bob was so scared he was about to wet himself. They quickly drove to a secluded spot several miles from town and dumped the body in a bushy ravine.

There wasn't ANY conversation at all on the way back to headquarters. They ushered a very anxious Bob into the Station and booked him into his usual room.

"What's the story on the armed robbery call?" the Sergeant questioned.

"Aw, it was just a false alarm," George muttered. "Didn't see a thing."

"Nope," Chip added. "Must have been a false alarm."

Donny couldn't believe what he'd just seen and heard. The realities of life on the street were a lot more than he'd bargained for, and he was having second thoughts about having anything to do with this profession.

"Well, false alarm or not, you still need to file a report," the Sergeant snapped.

Of course, being the rookie, Donny was assigned the job. You talk about confusion ... how in the world do you file a report on what had just happened? It was obvious he couldn't tell the truth, but how in the dickens was he supposed to handle THAT? He was left in a small interrogation room with the proper forms to fill out.

221

One can only imagine what was going through his mind. He kept stalling. If he told the truth, those maniacs might just whack him too, and if he lied he'd be an accessory to murder. Just as he was nearing mental collapse, the door opened and Chip and George entered the small room giggling. With them, was the also giggling "victim," still in his baseball cap and white shirt ... covered with the catsup stains from the packets that were broken in his pockets as he grabbed his chest and "died."

Everyone had a good laugh, and Donny was REALLY relieved to find out the truth. Whether it was an intentional oversight or not I don't know, but nobody ever bothered to let Bob in on the joke, and when they went to check on him in his cell he was sober as a judge. He just sat on the edge of the cot staring down between his shoes; not saying a word.

Maybe they ought to use that little trick more often, 'cause Bob hasn't been in a lick of trouble since. He dang shore doesn't want to have anything to do with those guys arrestin' HIM.

"Now, THAT"S a dirty trick."

Chapter Forty Six

Government Authority

One fine morning last June, Dick and Billy had finished the morning chores and were relaxin' on their ramshackle porch with a couple of bottles of whatever brand of liquid refreshment had been on sale the last time they were in town.

"That cranky ol' brockel faced cow with the busted horn finally calved last night," Billy offered between swigs.

"The one you call Hillary?" Dick questioned. "Dang it ... I was hopin' she was dry. That's gotta be the ugliest cow on the place."

"Can't say much for her attitude neither, she's a crabby ol' bag ... 'specially when she first calves. But, I'll tell you what ... she's dang shore a good mother. Ain't no coyote gonna pack off her baby, that's fer sure."

Dick squinted into the mid morning sun at a thin trail of dust rising from the rutted trail into their camp.

"Wonder who that is? Looks like we're gettin' company."

A few minutes later a car pulled into the yard with a little sign on the side that read; US Department of Agriculture, Statistical Division. A fat little guy that didn't look like he'd ever done a day's work stepped out.

"Good morning gentlemen. My name is Malcolm Pugsley," he said with an obvious air of importance. "I'm with the Statistics Division at the USDA. It appears you have failed to return the form you've been sent requesting that you report your livestock numbers and crop acreage information."

Just the thought of a government bureaucrat can get Billy's hackles up, and here's one standin' in his very own yard. "Nope," he answered matter-of-factly. "Ain't figurin' on sendin' it in, neither. That stuff ain't none of yer business."

"The gathering of statistics is vital in the formation of government policy," Mr. Pugsley curtly replied. "Failure to complete and return the form you were sent is a violation of the law."

"Law my foot!" Billy snorted, bristling as he stood. "I gotta mind to ..."

"Billy!" Dick quieted his old partner. "Jus' sit back down and relax. I'll handle this."

Dick went on to explain to their visitor that it was against their principles to divulge that information. They were upstanding taxpaying citizens and felt this was an unneeded invasion of their privacy. (Actually he didn't say it quite that eloquently, and he might have accidentally used a dirty word or two, but that was the gist of the conversation.)

Mr. Puglsey indignantly reached into the breast pocket of his black Sears & Roebuck polyester suit coat and flashed an official looking laminated card.

"I am authorized by law to conduct a personal survey of any agricultural operations in non compliance. Unless I'm given your permission to inspect the premises and calculate your livestock numbers personally, I will return with the proper law authorities, and you will be issued a citation for contempt."

"GGrrrr ... ," Billy growled as he stood again, his fists clenched tightly.

"Sit down, Billy!" Dick snapped. Again, Billy returned to his seat his glaring eyes never leaving the intruder's face.

"OK, OK ... ," Dick finally agreed. "We got nuthin' to hide anyway, so I guess it won't do no harm if you look around a little. Go ahead. You can leave your car here and walk. We don't want you drivin' around and wallerin' down all the grass. Just don't go in that pasture down by the creek."

"This gives me the authority to inspect ALL of your property," the government official snapped, again flashing the officially stamped and laminated card.

"Well, I wouldn't go in THAT field if I was you."

"Are you threatening me?" Mr. Pugsley questioned, looking authoritatively over his glasses, his fat little cheeks quivering and glistening with the heat of the mid morning sun.

"Nope ... no threats intended," Dick returned as calmly as possible.

"Fine ... then I'll take a few minutes to look around," Mr. Pugsley asserted victoriously, his demeanor reflecting an even greater air of importance. After retrieving a clipboard from the seat of his vehicle, the official inspector locked all the doors and walked straight towards the field in the willows by the creek ... the one containing the late calving cows.

"&%$#@# gover'ment jerks!" Billy was still fumin'. "Don't he have to have a warrant 'er somethin'? I thought this was America!"

"Jus' relax pardner," Dick chuckled as he handed him a fresh cold bottle of Milwaukee's finest. "I'm thinkin'maybe ol' Hillary might just cure that fella o' suckin' eggs ... an' here we got a ringside seat."

The boys weren't disappointed. They DID have a ringside seat there on the porch with a perfect view. Within five minutes there was a frightened yell for help (none was forthcoming) and the plainly distinguishable beller of a deranged cow on the prod. Back across the pasture as fast as his fat little legs would carry him came Mr. Pugsley, with Hillary encouraging his speed by a bellering little nudge in the seat of his fat little pants every other jump.

The boys where hoopin' and hollering encouragement and nearly giggled themselves right off their chairs. This was even better than the wild cow milkin' at the County Fair.

"Show her yer card, Mr. Pugsley! Just show her yer card!"

"Only thing that botherd me 'bout the deal was havin' Hillary runnin' with a full bag .... but I'd dang shore give a hu'nerd dollars to see THAT again."

Chapter Forty Seven

The Legend of "Long" George

*T*he reason George Francis got the nickname, "Long George" was obvious to anyone that ever laid an eye on him. He stood a slender six feet six inches tall in his stockin' feet, and in the high heeled riding boots and tall crowned Stetson he always wore, he definitely stood out in a crowd.

He was also famous for his fancy western clothes and the engraved pearl handled, nickel plated pistol at his side. Complete with a long legged, bay colored, trick horse by the name of Tony, and his silver mounted saddle gear, his appearance certainly helped to create the mystique that was, and indeed still is, "Long George."

George Mortimer Francis was born September 21, 1874 at Camp Floyd, Cedar Valley, Utah. He came to the Milk River country of northern Montana in 1893 at the age of eighteen on a cattle train with the Warbonnet Livestock Company. They had been previously running on the Fort Hall Indian Reservation in southern Idaho, but were crowded out by the influx of settlers, and headed for Montana to the last of the open range. The cattle were unloaded at Box Elder, and trailed to the rich grass of the Clear Creek valley on the northern slope of the Bear Paw Mountains.

Long George spent the rest of his life in northern

Montana, and became something of a folk hero. Quite the showman, he was instrumental in organizing and producing rodeos, the most notable of which was the Great Northern Stampede in Havre. Many of George's exploits (on both sides of the law) were written up in national papers, including the New York Herald, and were also featured on many radio stations. A story of his life was considered for a movie in the early days of motion pictures, and was the subject of a 1989 book entitled, Tall In the Saddle, The Long George Francis Story, by Montana historian Gary A. Wilson. The book was later republished by Globe Pequot Press and entitled, Long George Francis, Gentleman Outlaw of Montana.

Long George The Gentleman

Long George competed in many rodeos, some as far away as the prestigious Pendleton Roundup, in both the bull dogging and steer roping events. His bay horse Tony would put the finishing touches on his steer roping performances by placing one front hoof on the steer's ribs and taking a bow, to the glee of the appreciative audience.

George was a good hand with cattle and horses, and although a flashy dressing showman, he was also a rather shy but extremely likeable man with a ready smile and a host of loyal friends. It wasn't all sunshine however, as there were many rumors about his "long rope" and the fact that more than a few of the cattle and horses that he traded were not strictly his own.

Long George & Tony

"Mavericking," or branding slick calves missed by the roundup wagons in the Fall gathers was a common practice, but rumors persisted that George maybe didn't wait until the roundup was over, and hurried along the weaning process a little by just helping himself to other folks' stock on a regular basis. His expertise with a rope no doubt added fuel to the rumors.

His real forte though was horses, and the demand for all types of horse flesh was at its peak in the early 1900's. Long George had a reputation for being a top horse trainer, and of course, abundant innuendo concerning the suspected means by which he'd obtained the many horses he traded continued to flourish.

Such a reputation is bound to gain a man a few enemies in addition to his many faithful friends, and he

229

accumulated more of each with every passing year. He was soon considered by many to be the leader of an organized band of cattle and horse thieves that operated statewide as well as in all of the adjoining states and Canadian Provinces. If ever an animal came up missing, "Long George" got the blame.

He was eventually charged with stealing a horse from one of his powerful enemies, and a warrant for his arrest, along with a $500 reward was issued. George maintained his innocence, saying that he was being framed for spite. The resulting trial was quite a spectacle, with an ending that was widely reported by an Eastern reporter, and several "eyewitnesses" (that were nowhere around). The newspaper account may have been baloney, but it was certainly befitting any Wild West movie.

The report was that when the jury came in with a verdict of guilty, Long George produced a pistol that had been slipped to him by one of his many faithful friends, and holding the entire courtroom in his sights, backed to an open window, whistled for his horse Tony, and galloped away to freedom.

That IS a good story, but a long ways from the truth. George was convicted, but just didn't show up at his sentencing hearing, and instead went into hiding, spending quite a length of time holed up in the Bear Paw Mountains, a fugitive from justice.

The death of Long George was also a mystery fit for the finest of the pulp fiction detective magazines, and the stories surrounding it (with varying degrees of accuracy) flourished. He died in a severe blizzard with the thermometer registering a chilling 22 degrees below zero on Christmas Eve of 1920.

He was making his way to spend the holiday with his fiancé who was teaching at a country school several miles northwest of Havre. With the visibility standing at near zero due to the storm, his 1914 Hupmobile slid off a cut bank and onto the ice of the Milk River. George was badly injured in the rollover crash with a compound leg fracture and head injuries.

With any rescue on the wind swept prairie certainly not coming in time to keep him from freezing to death, he crudely splinted the broken leg and made an attempt to get to a house that he knew was a mile or two away. After a valiant effort, dragging

the broken leg through the snow, the blood loss took its toll, and it was clear to the nearly frozen cowboy that this was the end of the trail. With his pistol back down the blood soaked trail in the wrecked car and his energy completely spent, Long George Francis remained the master of his own destiny.

Rather than risk being found alive by predators, he used the last strength he could muster to plunge

231

his pocket knife into his jugular vein, taking his own life. Ironically, had the cowboy been horseback, he probably would have survived the trip, served his time in the Montana State Prison, and then returned to marry his sweetheart as he'd promised.

"Long George" Francis was indeed a genuine folk hero in northern Montana, and like all folk heroes, the stories of his many exploits in life and the extraordinary circumstances of his death were told and retold by friend and foe alike, changing a little with every telling. Many of his loyal friends maintained to their graves that his death wasn't suicide at all, but that he was indeed murdered by his powerful enemies.

Editor's Note: The entire compelling story of Long George Francis has been tediously and accurately researched and compiled by Montana historian Gary A. Wilson in his book, Long George Francis, Gentleman Outlaw of Montana, published by Globe Pequot Press.

Chapter

Forty Eight

Buyin' 'em Right

"Floyd? ... this is Jim," the old cowpuncher mumbled into the telephone. (He always did hate them durn things ... at least he didn't get one of those new-fangled answerin' machines. He ALWAYS just hangs up on those.)

"Oh, yea ... Hi, Jim, how 'r things goin' over there?" Floyd returned.

"Purty good I guess. I was wonderin' if maybe you could spare a couple hours to give me a hand tomorrow mornin'. The vet's comin' out to preg test the heifers and I could sure use a little help if you ain't too busy."

"Sure. I ain't got that much goin' on around here. If I stay home I'll just find somethin' that needs fixin' and it'll cost me money. It's way cheaper to just help you."

"Will ten o'clock work?"

"Yup ... I'll be there."

"Good ... thanks ... see you tomorrow."

Click.

Jim never was a fella that liked to talk on the phone all that much.

The next mornin' as Floyd came rattlin' in Jim's yard with his pickup and trailer, the heifers were already in the corral behind the squeeze chute, and the boys barely had time to say good mornin' before the vet topped the hill in a big cloud of dust. Those guys always seem to be in a hurry for some reason.

Jim and Floyd are next door neighbors, and as is the usual custom out here in the Real West, they trade work back and forth without either one of them botherin' to keep track of who owes who what. If the rest of the world operated like that there'd sure be a lot fewer problems than there are.

They were soon all strung out, with Jim up running the chute and Floyd on the left side poking them up the alleyway. As usual, there was a fairly large amount of BS floating back and forth.

"You sure y' got all the steers out o' here?" Floyd joshed.

"It's too late now," the Doc teased back. "Just bring 'em on up here. I preg test steers too ... and it doesn't cost a dime more."

One of the best parts about working with a crew is the good natured baloney that goes with the job, and there was plenty of it that morning. Things were going well. When you've got a decent setup and a good crew sometimes things just work.

"Hey, Jim ... here comes one that lost her ear tag," Floyd hollered.

234

Jim quickly walked back down the alley to take a look. "Ah ... ," he muttered under his breath as he shook his head and peered between the boards. "I pulled that one's tag out. That's the worst dang heifer on the place. I don't know what I was thinkin' about when I saved her. I ain't sure what to do with that scrub. I guess we oughta eat 'er, but we just killed a beef and the freezer's full."

Jim's a good cowman, and Floyd has a lot of respect for his opinion, but he sure couldn't see anything so wrong with her. She was a big black Angus with good flesh and a nice long back. In fact, she looked pretty good to him.

"You gonna take 'er to the sale barn?"

"Are you kiddin'? An' let all the neighbors see what kind o' scrub cattle I got? I got more pride than that."

Floyd took another long look at her standing there in the alleyway, and even with a second glance, she sure looked OK to him. There's an old horse tradin' secret that Floyd's known since he was a kid. It's always a lot cheaper to buy a critter from a fella that wants rid of it, and it was a cinch that Jim was a well motivated seller.

"So what d' ya want for her?" Floyd dangled the bait in front of his neighbor's nose.

"Oh, you don't want that dang thing," Jim countered. "She ain't worth haulin' home."

"Holy cow," Floyd thought to himself, giving the heifer yet another long look. The dollar signs were starting to float around in his hat, and he could almost taste the profit now. He STILL couldn't see anything wrong with her."

"Well, I'll admit she ain't all THAT good," he finally said slyly, "but we got a little extra grass ... what would you take for her?"

"I don't know what you'd want a dink heifer like that for," Jim mumbled, shaking his head again and looking at the ground. "But I sure want rid of her. I'll take five hundred bucks if you haul her home today."

"FIVE HUNDRED BUCKS?" Floyd cunningly hid his grin as he repeated the price to himself. "She's worth at least twice that," he thought.

"Ah ... OK ... , I guess I'll take 'er," he said with just the right amount of hesitation. "Doc, just go ahead and test her."

"Good deal," Jim said smugly. "I was wonderin' how I was gonna get rid o' that dang thing. Just back yer trailer up here to the squeeze chute an' we'll load her right up."

"She's an early calver," the vet yelled from his vantage point on her south end.

Floyd was having a hard time keeping a straight face. This was the best deal he'd gotten into in a LONG time. He REALLY hated to take advantage of a good neighbor like that ... but then Jim had named his own price.

It wasn't until the heifer had jumped into the trailer and turned around that Floyd figured out why Jim was so anxious to sell her. When she swapped ends there it was ... plastered all over her ribs ... a nice big plain triangle J brand on her right side ... Floyd's very own brand.

"I'll be waitin' fer that check," Jim grinned. "Looks like you won't even have to re-brand her."

That Ol' Jim's a pretty hard fella to sneak up on.

236

"Doggone it, Billy. Looks like this dang book is about out o' pages. If there's ain't any more stories, then we're gonna have t' go back t' work."

"Yea, guess so. ... Boy, hate that. ... but then I've 'bout got m' breakfast over with anyhow."

Home

How long's it been since these old walls
   have heard a Mother's labor sigh

How many years since through my halls
   have rung a baby's bornin' cry

Well, just this mornin' before the sun
   breached that eastern hill

I heard that sweet song once again
   from my window sill

For most of a hundred years I've stood
   beside this little stream

Drawn many families to my breast
   as they embrace their dreams

The men folk come and work the land
   'til they're no longer young

And I've from my humble kitchen heard
   a million tunes be hummed

Oh, my timbers hold such secrets
   but you know they're safe with me

And I've heard a million prayers or two
   at night from bended knee

Oh, how I wish my builder
  his final race long run

I wish that he could see me now
  to behold what I've become

For when with skillful hand and strong
  he lay stone on stone

He just thought he built a house ...

But I've Become a Home

*Written in Honor of
Faith Karleen Halingstad
Born here in our home ... April 19, 1998*

Ken Overcast

*K*en Overcast is a busy guy, and VERY seldom gets to sit in his old rockin' chair. He and his wife Dawn (alias Miss Apple Pie in this book), ranch on Lodge Creek in north central Montana, where they have a commercial cow herd.

Ken is also an entertainer and author as well as being a cowboy, and travels throughout the West singing songs and telling stories. He has recorded several CD's of what he likes to describe as "cowboy music." This is his fourth book of stories, and probably won't be his last, because as he says ...

"I've still got a few more that need tellin'."

Ken began producing a weekly radio program entitled, *The Cowboy Show, with Ken Overcast* several years ago that is syndicated from coast to coast, and also writes a couple of syndicated columns that appear in regional and national publications.

www.kenovercast.com

Sittin' 'Round
The Stove

*Stories From the
Real West*

by

Ken Overcast

Bear Valley Press

BVP

Ken Overcast is available to entertain
at your gatherings or special events.
Real Music and Real Stories from the Real West.

Cover Painting of the Overcast Boys
H. Steven Oiestad

Rear Cover Photo
Judy Stegmeier

Illustrated by
Ben Crane

Chapter Heading Photo
Roy Matheson & Honky Tom
Chinook, Montana 1904
Charles E. Morris

Copyright © 2008 Ken Overcast
All rights Reserved

Library of Congress Control Number: 2008909504

Printed in Canada
First Edition
First Printing
ISBN-13: 978-0-9718481-3-9
ISBN-10: 0-9718481-3-0

Bear Valley Press
PO Box 1542
Chinook, Montana 59523
406-357-3824

www.kenovercast.com

4